BOUND

THE BILLIONAIRE'S MUSE 2

M. S. PARKER

BELMONTE PUBLISHING, LLC

Copyright © 2017 Belmonte Publishing LLC

Published by Belmonte Publishing LLC

ISBN-13: 978-1979048224

ISBN-10: 1979048223

1

SINE

"*You'll miss the sea.*"

When I had told my family I was leaving Ireland to go to DeVry University in America, that was the first thing my dad said. He was right. I did miss it, but as much as I loved my seaside place of birth, I'd found a home here in New York City. A permanent home, I hoped.

I could only hope this new job would allow me to stay here. I had no more desire to live in Ireland and join my family's whiskey business than I did when I'd left five years ago. While I loved my family, I couldn't deny that it was freeing not being known as the baby of the McNiven eight.

The problem was, I needed a full-time job to be able to transfer from a temporary visa to a permanent, but I didn't have any better idea of what I wanted to do with my business administration degree than I did the day I had declared my major. It seemed like a solid choice at the time, the sort of thing that would provide for me financially while I found my passion. Instead, I'd spent the last year working as a temp at a variety of jobs around Manhattan.

I had done well as a temp. I worked hard, gave a hundred percent, and it rarely took me long to learn the various tasks. On top of that, I was easy to get along with. More or less. I wasn't the type of woman who intimidated other women or sparked jealousy. Most looked at me as a little sister, especially since I barely looked eighteen, much less twenty-three. That meant I could navigate through the petty spats that often dragged down newcomers. I made sure I was polite and added to small talk when appropriate, but I never did inane chatting that interfered with my work.

More than one employer had told me they wished they were able to hire me permanently. I'd always appreciated the compliment as I walked out the door for the last time.

I'd never mind moving from place to place, but after a year of bouncing around, I was looking forward to a change of pace.

And today was the day. Everything could change for the better.

As I stood outside the Chelsea studio of my new employer, I said a quick prayer to St. Cajetan and took a deep breath. I didn't consider myself a religious person, but Mam was devout, so all us kids had been baptized into the church. I hoped that carried some weight with the patron saint of jobs, even if I didn't completely believe in all that.

I needed all the help I could get.

I knocked on the door and ran through everything I knew about my new job while I waited. It wasn't much.

On Friday, I'd been called into the agency for an interview with a woman named Jean Holloman. She was an agent looking for an assistant to a photographer she represented, and I'd been recommended for the position. Ms. Holloman hadn't said why or by who, but I knew better than to look a gift horse in the mouth. After a brief chat, she'd given me this address and ordered me to be there at nine o'clock sharp. I'd be working for Alix Wexler.

The way she said his name made me think that she assumed I knew who he was. I hadn't bothered to tell her otherwise. If this position meant I didn't have to start looking for another roommate – or another apartment – or a plane ticket back to Ireland – Mr. Wexler could be an *abhartach,* and I would still have accepted the job.

The door opened, and I heard a voice telling me to come inside, but whoever it was had already moved back into the shadows. I followed, blinking as my eyes adjusted from the bright June sun to the dimmer interior of the studio. I could see the outline of a man, over a foot taller than my own barely five-foot frame, but wasn't able to make out the details until I followed him into a large, open space filled with natural light.

Messy dark brown hair, and a chiseled jaw any sculpture would have loved. When he turned to face me, my stomach did a flip. His features and build were attractive enough that I was sure he turned heads wherever he went, but it was those eyes that made me catch my breath. I'd never seen irises quite that color before. They were gray, but not a washed out blue, but rather the thicker, darker color I associated with smoke curling up from a chimney on a cold day.

"You're my new assistant, right?" His voice was clipped, but he didn't seem to be angry as much as distracted.

I tried not to be offended. I wasn't here for a date or for a business meeting. He was my new boss. He could be as distracted as he wanted. I'd get paid either way.

"Yes, sir. I'm Sine McNiven."

That got his attention, though I wasn't sure if it was my accent or my name. His gaze swept over me, and I got the impression that it was the first time he actually saw me. I did my best not to fidget.

"You want to give me that one again?"

I tempered my grin. Wouldn't want the boss thinking I was laughing at him. "S-I-N-E, but it's pronounced SHEE-na. Rhymes with Tina."

"And you're old enough to be my assistant?"

Not the first time I'd heard that question in some form or another. "Don't you know it's not polite to ask a woman her age?" I smiled as I added, "But I'm twenty-three."

"Are you now?" He raised an eyebrow. "Where are you from?"

I was tempted to say Queens, but I knew what he

meant. "Balbriggan." When he raised the second eyebrow, I added, "Ireland."

He looked like he was debating whether or not to ask anything else, then he shrugged. "Follow me."

I looked around as he started walking toward the back of the studio. Mrs. Holloman had told me that he was a photographer, but not how talented he was. If he was the one who'd taken the pictures hanging on the walls, he had talent. I wasn't an expert, but even I could tell these were good. I didn't offer my opinion though, not knowing Mr. Wexler well enough to know how he'd take it. Artists could be mercurial.

"This is your office." He pushed open the door and stepped out of the way to let me inside. "Feel free to spend today getting it organized."

"Is there anything you need me to do today?" I asked.

"Jean's the one who thinks I need an assistant," he said, and I could almost feel him roll his eyes. "I just didn't feel like arguing."

I watched as he walked away and reminded myself again that artists were often temperamental, and that indifferent was far better than angry. Besides, I'd grown up with six brothers. I could handle one moody man.

2

ALIX

I'd known Jean Holloman all my life. She'd been a friend of my mother's since they were teenagers, so she was a staple at holidays and birthday parties over the years. When I told my parents I wanted to be a photographer, they'd told me I needed an agent. And then my mom called Jean. She'd been my agent ever since.

I was used to Jean doing whatever she thought was best for me, often without telling me first, and it usually didn't bother me, but this time, she'd gone too far.

I wasn't a morning person, never had been, and she knew it, so when I saw her number on my caller ID at seven in the morning, I'd assumed it was something important.

"I hired an assistant."

I frowned. Not important. Certainly not important enough to wake me up this fucking early. Jean said something that could have been a name, but I didn't really care. "Good for you. Enjoy."

"She'll be at your studio at nine. Don't be an ass."

And then she hung up.

What the hell? I mentally cursed her for a couple more minutes, then got up to make myself some coffee since I knew I'd never get back to sleep, not when I was trying to figure out how to politely get out of the mess Jean had gotten me into. I didn't need an assistant. I didn't want one.

I'd been having a hard-enough time with my art lately. I didn't need someone watching me fail.

When I heard the knock at the door at five minutes before nine, I knew it was her. Jean had told me her name, but I hadn't been awake enough to register it. Not that it mattered. I'd give her a couple days, and then let Jean know that I was fine on my own.

I probably sounded like an ass when I told her to come in, but it wasn't until she said her name that I really looked at her.

And wondered if my eyes were playing tricks on me, because there was no way Jean had hired a kid, and this girl didn't look old enough to be out of high school. She was short, first off, barely five feet tall, and she had this mass of orange-red curls that went with her freckles. But then she grinned at me, and I found myself wanting to smile back. Her eyes were impossibly green, and they sparkled.

Like seriously fucking sparkled.

So I talked to her. Only a couple questions, but it was

more than I'd planned on asking. There was something about her that piqued my interest. I didn't let it take over though. Sine could be the best assistant in the world, and it wouldn't change anything. I didn't need her help. I liked my privacy as much as possible.

I left her in her office but kept thinking about her as I went back to the main room of my studio. I'd just finished up a series of landscape and nature photos, so they were up on my walls now, but I'd only shot them because I felt the need to take a break from my usual subjects. I'd been feeling burned out and had hoped that the change of pace would get me back on track.

It hadn't.

I walked to the table where I kept all my equipment. I had a model coming in shortly, and I needed to start preparing, but I couldn't focus.

I needed to decide on a theme, set up the appropriate props and backlighting...but the only thing I could picture in my mind's eye was the redhead I could hear moving around a few yards away. She was pretty enough that most men would probably give her a smile if she walked by, but she wasn't the sort of beautiful that would turn heads.

Still, the lines of her face had fascinated me, and I found myself thinking about the way shadows would play across her cheeks, her lips. How I'd position her so that the light would hit her. The way the sun would shine against her curls.

I frowned.

Sine wasn't a model. She was too short, for one thing.

She'd dressed nice, but I got the feeling it was just because she wanted to appear proper, not because she was trying to impress me.

Which I found odd.

Women always wanted to impress me. I wasn't bragging. There were the women who wanted me for my name and my family's money, and then the women who were into me because of the whole artsy thing. They wanted me to hire them as models. But Sine had smiled without flirting and had showed no interest in anything beyond her tasks.

Okay, she's only been here less than an hour, but I'd once had a pizza delivery girl give me her phone number after telling me that she'd been trying to break into modeling *forever*.

I appreciated it though, even if I didn't understand it. If Sine had come in, hinting around to model or been flirty, I probably would've sent her away immediately, and had a firmer word with Jean about not needing an assistant. Since she'd been professional so far, maybe I should at least give Sine a chance before I told Jean I was right.

Sine.

I shook my head. How in the world did *S-I-N-E* rhyme with *Tina*?

"Alix, darling, so sorry I'm late."

I didn't have to look to know that my model had just walked in. Giselle Lucan had been posing for me for two weeks, but I hadn't been satisfied with any of the shots. She was gorgeous, of course, with perfect skin and features to go with ebony hair and china blue eyes. *She* was a woman who didn't merely turn heads. At twenty-two, she'd already been engaged three times to rich men who'd lavished her with gifts until she'd gotten bored with them. The fact that this was her reputation should have been my warning to steer clear of her, but I was doing a line of erotic photography, and Giselle oozed the sexuality I thought would sell.

If I could find my footing again.

3

SINE

Mr. Wexler might not have thought he needed an assistant, but one look at the office he said was mine told me that his agent had a clearer view of things than he did.

I put my hands on my hips and tried to figure out where to start. I'd always been an organized person. Da said it came from me needing to prove my capability for independence. Mam said it was because none of the men in our family had an organized bone in their body and needed us women to keep the business from falling apart.

A familiar twinge went through my heart. Seven siblings, and I was the only one who'd chosen to leave. Mam and Aileen took care of the books while the boys and Da did the heavy lifting and the marketing. The whiskey business had been in Da's family for generations, and all of us kids knew that Mam's family had encouraged the match because of it. A part of me still wished I'd been able to find happiness there like my siblings had.

I took a deep breath and set my jaw. This wasn't the time or place to be thinking maudlin thoughts. I had a job to do.

Trash would be the first to go, I decided. Things that were obvious. Then I'd work through each of the numerous piles of papers and letters one by one, throwing away the junk and separating the rest into categories.

I'd need to get a calendar, work on writing down Mr. Wexler's schedule, but I needed to sort through the important things first so that I could make sure he didn't miss anything.

I'd worked as a temp for more than one executive who knew the things they wanted to do but forgot bills that needed to be paid, or their mother-in-law's birthdays. I didn't know if Mr. Wexler had a mother-in-law, but I knew there were plenty of other things he could be forgetting, and it was my job to make sure that didn't happen.

I found a trash can next to the desk and got to work.

I had to admit, when I was told my new boss was a photographer, I was a little worried that he'd be the stereotypical artist. Back home, my one and only sister had dated an artist for six months her freshman year of college. Aileen was fifteen years older than me, so I didn't remember the guy, but he'd been enough of a bastard that when I was in high school, my entire family had warned me against ever dating an artist. Fortunately, Aileen met

Roger a few months later, and they'd been together ever since.

Still, I'd always been wary of finding *another Eugene*. Artists were moody, often using drugs and alcohol to self-medicate. They slept around. Fickle. Volatile. All words Mam had used to describe Eugene.

So, as I went around the room looking for trash, I prepared myself to find beer cans, empty bottles of hard liquor, bags of drugs, pills.

Except I didn't find any of that.

A few fast food wrappers had missed the trashcan – probably because it was overflowing – and there were a couple empty bottles labeled with the name of some energy drink, but most of the junk I found was exactly that. Junk. Advertisements, credit card offers, that sort of thing.

As I made a pile of things that needed to be shredded, the phone on the desk rang. I picked it up and reminded myself to speak slowly. "Good morning. Alix Wexler's studio. Miss McNiven speaking."

"You managed to get into the studio and he's letting you answer the phone. Good work."

I blinked. I could tell it was a woman, but that was about it. "May I ask who's calling?"

"It's Jean Holloman, Miss NcNiven."

"Oh, good morning, Ms. Holloman." I'd only spoken to her the once when I'd been hired. "If you'll hold for a moment, I'll get Mr. Wexler."

"I didn't call to talk to him," she said. Her tone was

brusque, but I had the impression that was simply her way. "I wanted to know how you were doing."

"I'm well," I said. "I've started organizing the office."

Ms. Holloman barked a laugh. "Good luck with that. Alix doesn't know shit about organization."

"It's a good thing you hired me then," I said.

"That part's needed," she said. "But there's something more important that I need you to do. It's why I called you."

I glanced toward the door. Something in her voice made me wonder if Alix knew about this conversation.

"Alix is rich."

All right, that wasn't exactly what I'd been expecting.

"Not like owning a Mercedes and a home in the Hamptons rich, but the sort of rich that could probably maintain the economy of a small country."

I leaned back against the desk, suddenly light-headed. I'd already thought I would be out of my depth here, but that revelation made it painfully clear. I hoped Ms. Holloman didn't think I was going to try to–

"The reason I hired you is because I knew you wouldn't look at Alix and see a meal ticket," she continued. "In fact, I need you to protect him from people who'd take advantage of him, try to cheat him out of what's his."

I nodded, then remembered she couldn't see me. "Of course."

"If you think someone's going to do that, and you don't think he'll listen to you, I want you to call me. Will you do that?"

"I will."

"Good."

And then the call was done.

My head spun as I shuffled papers on the desk, my hands needing something to do. I'd need to shred even more of these things than I'd thought. I couldn't risk anyone finding something they could use to steal his identity. I would be his assistant...and his protector.

I walked over to the door of the office and looked out to where Mr. Wexler was staring at one of his photos.

He seemed...intense.

I didn't know why that particular photo captured his attention, but whatever the reason, he seemed to be caught up in those thoughts. I turned back to the office, knowing I couldn't spend the day watching him, trying to figure out the type of man he truly was. I supposed I'd find out soon enough.

If he didn't fire me first.

Which meant I needed to make sure I was invaluable.

So I went back to work.

I realized Mr. Wexler had a strange sort of order to his things. I'd always had a knack for seeing patterns, which sometimes gave me a different insight, and now, it was showing me that he was more organized than I initially gave him credit for. Not that it would appear that way to someone who couldn't find the order under the chaos. Since my new job was to keep things in order, I decided to make my own filing system, but first I needed to clear out a few items laying around the office before lunch.

I picked up the various lens and parts, putting them all into a now empty box, then took a deep breath. As I stepped into the studio, the first thing I noticed was the lighting had changed, but it wasn't because it was now early afternoon.

He was working.

He had an entire set up of lighting equipment with names I didn't know and was moving around the pile of pillows at their center. His back was to me, but I could read the intensity coming off him in waves. I couldn't even imagine being the focus of that sort of intensity, that...passion.

I couldn't imagine *having* that sort of passion.

If my time at the temp agency had taught me anything, it was that a difference existed between a job I didn't mind doing and one about which I was passionate. I'd seen that sort of purpose with my brothers for the family business, but I'd yet to have found my own.

As Mr. Wexler stepped to the side, I saw the subject of his focus.

An absolutely gorgeous woman.

Who was wearing very little.

Apparently, landscapes weren't the only thing in which he was interested.

4

ALIX

Six fucking hours wasted.

It wasn't Giselle's fault. She was gorgeous and willing to do whatever I wanted. She'd made *that* exceptionally clear, even though I always made sure my models knew it when they signed their contracts that I wasn't part of a benefits package. She'd handled my subtle rejection well, but it hadn't made any difference to the utter failure of the shoot.

I'd changed the lighting. Arranged and re-arranged the pillows she'd posed on. Gave her different costumes to wear, if those bits of lace and ribbon could be considered costumes. She'd looked amazing in them, each curve and dip of her body perfectly sensuous. But as gorgeous as she'd looked, I couldn't capture the pure and true essence that made the difference between erotic art and pornography.

Erotic photography had been my bread and butter for

years. Well, that wasn't entirely true, since I had a trust fund so large that the interest alone was enough for me to live off comfortably for decades to come. Add to that my cousin Izett's knack for wise investments and my eventual inheritance, I could've gotten away with never working a day in my life.

Maybe I'd taken my gift as far as it could go. Giselle was a new model for me, but I still felt like the photos were repetitive. Technically, they were perfect, exactly like all the others I'd taken. That was the problem. Like the landscapes hanging on the walls of my studio, they were beautiful, but not inspired. I could probably still get paid decent money for them, but I felt like I'd lost the sense of true art.

I pushed all that aside as I flashed my membership card at the doorman, giving him a polite smile as I stepped past. I wasn't at Gilded Cage to wallow. I needed stress relief. If I was lucky, it would be enough to help me find my footing again.

I was late, so the others were already here. I made my way through the crowd to our usual table. The oldest of the group, Jace Randell, was already scanning the crowd, looking for a partner for the night. Like me, he wasn't interested in relationships, but rather a pleasurable encounter without any strings.

My cousin, Erik Sanders, had been like that up until recently when he'd fallen for a sweet girl named Tanya Lacey. I'd never thought I'd see my cousin ready to settle down, but even after only a month, I could see that he was captivated. It'd been a rocky start for the two of them, but this past weekend, I heard things had changed. Erik had wanted us to meet tonight to fill us in on what happened.

Erik's former college roommate, Reb Union, had a girl-friend, but he hadn't brought her to the club the last few weeks. That, plus his recent increase in alcohol consumption made me think that things might not be going as well as they had been. I hated to see my friend hurting, but I couldn't say I'd be sorry to see Mitzi go. None of us really liked her.

"Running late?" Erik asked as I took the open seat next to him. "I ordered you a Highland Park."

I nodded my thanks and turned my attention to my cousin as he filled us in on what'd happened since last time.

Listening to his story, I was half-way through my second glass when I eyed a slim redhead on the dance floor. She reminded me of Sine for some reason. Maybe the hair.

As soon as Erik announced he was leaving – he was expecting a call from Tanya – Jace excused himself to find whoever had caught his eyes. When Reb told me he was about ready to leave, I decided to go after the redhead.

Gilded Cage wasn't your typical club you would visit to dance and pick up women. It was a BDSM club that catered to those of us in the lifestyle. Not only was this a safe place to express our sexual preferences without fear of judgment, it also offered rooms VIP members, such as myself and my friends, could enjoy without having to arrange a private space ahead of time. All four of us were

Doms, though we each had different taste when it came to whom we found attractive as well as the particular aspects of our preferred role.

The redhead had kept her eye on me as she danced, so as soon as I started toward her, she stopped and ducked her head, assuming one of the usual positions a Sub would take when meeting an unknown Dom.

I was glad she had at least some experience. I wasn't in the mood for introductory lessons tonight. We'd have a quick chat to ensure we were both on the same page, then set up our safe word before I took her back to one of the rooms. The routine was familiar, comfortable. The prelude to a few enjoyable couple of hours.

MANY PEOPLE outside the lifestyle think that everyone into BDSM enjoys the same things: handcuffs, whips, leather, and chains. The recent influx of modern romance books and movies with their bossy alpha males hadn't helped change that impression. Sure, I knew plenty of Doms who were into all that but not me. No, my preferences leaned toward artistic bondage. Ropes and scarves caught my attention.

Which was why Rae would be trussed up on the massive bed that took up most of the far wall. As soon as we'd stepped into the room, I'd told her to strip, but there hadn't been much for her to take off. Her tight, tiny dress had been the *only* thing she'd been wearing. Once it was off, she stood with her hands clasped behind her back and let me look her over.

Small breasts that were barely a handful, with tight pink nipples. A bare pussy, with the tattoo of a butterfly right above it. The name *Rae* at the small of her back in fancy script, which meant she was using her real name. No piercings or scars.

Once I positioned her on her stomach on the bed, I opened one of the drawers beneath it and pulled out a series of silk ropes. They were softer than regular ropes, and more colorful, which was what I wanted.

I turned on the speaker that pumped the club music in, so even though neither of us spoke, the room wasn't silent. I let my fingers trail across her skin as I positioned her just the way I wanted, and her eyes followed my every move. I slid my hand under her, ran my thumb across one hard nipple, and saw her shiver. She whimpered as I parted her legs, brushed my fingers against her damp core.

When I finished, I stepped back to admire my work. Her legs were spread and bent, tied with the rope. I'd bound her arms behind her back too, then connected wrists to ankles. The colors of the rope showed up nicely against her skin. A perfect image.

Perfect image...

That was when it clicked.

I'd taken erotic photographs, but never anything like this. Granted, I'd never done anything quite so explicit, but this could be a good idea.

Rae wriggled on the bed, reminding me that this wasn't

the time or place to be musing on my artistic issues. I could figure that out later.

Right now, I had a naked Sub on the bed in front of me, and a body full of tension that needed release.

I walked around to the other side of the bed and moved onto my knees in front of her. I reached up and grabbed a pillow, arranging it under her chest to raise her up enough to keep her from getting a crick in her neck. Some controlled pain was one thing, but general pain was something else. Some Doms might have liked to make their Subs uncomfortable, but that wasn't my thing. I never kept my Subs bound beyond what was necessary. I was all about the look and the control, not the pain. Not that I'd ever judge those who were into the more masochism side of the lifestyle. It just wasn't me.

I brushed some hair away, stroked my thumb down the side of her face, let it brush the corner of her mouth. She wasn't wearing much make-up, which was a plus. I always preferred the natural look, the more minimalist, the better. She was beautiful without it. High cheekbones and big eyes. She had the sort of lips I couldn't wait to see wrapped around my cock.

For a moment, I had a flash of another set of lips, ones curving into a teasing smile, and wondered what it would feel like to have *those* in front of me.

I pushed the errant thought aside and reached into my pocket for a condom. Rae licked her lips as she watched me unzip my pants. I didn't take them off. I rarely did when I was here. It was just sex.

I pressed my thumb against the seam of her mouth. She sucked it into her mouth, flicked her tongue against the tip, and I made a sound in the back of my throat. I rolled on the protection and put my hand on the back of her head, holding her in place as I guided my erection between her lips.

Her mouth was hot and wet, even through the latex, and I flexed my fingers in her hair. Shallow thrusts mingled with incredible suction had my balls drawing up, pleasure coiling at the base of my spine. She knew what she was doing.

I let the sensations wash over me until, finally, I backed away, sliding from her mouth with a faint popping sound. Her breathing was harsh, but as I moved around behind her, I could see how wet she was. Still, I slipped my fingers between her legs, parting her until I could stroke her already swollen clit. Even as I moved from making firm circles over that bundle of nerves to sliding two fingers into her cunt, I had the eerie feeling of deja vu, like this was something I'd done so many times that it had become rote.

"May I come, Sir?"

The question snapped my attention from the strange path my thoughts had been taking.

"Please, Sir."

I could hear the strain in her voice as she tried to stop herself from squirming, and I twisted my fingers, searching for that sweet spot inside her.

"You may come when you're ready," I said as I brushed my knuckles against her g-spot.

Her pussy tightened around my fingers as she shuddered. She was strangely quiet as she came, but there was no mistaking the pleasure in her voice as she breathed, "Thank you, Sir."

I grasped her forearms, using them for leverage as I slid inside her. She felt good wrapped around me, rocking back to meet each thrust. I set a steady pace that was neither too fast nor too slow. I didn't want to drag out the experience, but I also wanted to make her climax again. I was a firm believer in the power of positive reinforcement, and nothing said *you did well* like an orgasm. And she'd earned at least two of them.

After several minutes, I increased my speed, shifting her body until I rubbed against her g-spot with every stroke. It wasn't long before she came again, this time letting out a groan as her muscles squeezed me. I swore, eyes closing as I followed.

And for those several brief seconds, I forgot about my pushy agent sending me an assistant. Forgot about my lack of inspiration. Forgot about how this was just another physical release with absolutely nothing else behind it.

5

SINE

Three days.

That's how long it had taken to organize the office, and then all day yesterday to get Alix's bills and payment schedules synced with his appointments so that everything was all in one place. We'd had a bit of a row on Wednesday when I'd asked about handling his bills. He'd insisted he was an adult and fully capable of paying his bills himself. It probably would have escalated to the point where I would've said something I shouldn't have, but in the middle of it all, as if God was sending a message, the lights went out.

He hadn't apologized when I politely informed him that the electric company hadn't received his payment...or when I confirmed that he'd paid his bill for his city apartment twice. He had, however, told me to call him Alix instead of Mr. Wexler, so I'd counted it a win.

With a bowl of cereal in my hand, I scowled as I looked

at myself in my bathroom mirror. I'd made the mistake yesterday of taking advantage of the June sunshine after work and had gone for a run in Central Park. The run hadn't been the mistake, but not buying stronger sunscreen was. I didn't burn as badly as I could have, but my nose and cheeks were redder than I liked. With fair skin like mine, burns and more freckles were the only response to the sun, but this looked more like I was blushing, and I didn't want Alix to think I was embarrassed by the subject of his photographs.

I'd been very careful not to show any reaction to the photographs he was taking or to the way his model pranced around half-naked. I wasn't paid to be an art critic or his conscience. My job was to make sure the lights stayed on, and he didn't double-book.

I put the bowl down and smoothed foundation over the sensitive skin, taking care to blend the edges. I rarely wore makeup, but I felt like representing a photographer meant being a bit more aware of how I looked. Alix hadn't said a word to me about my attire, but I'd seen the looks Giselle had sent my way every afternoon when she saw me. I didn't care what she thought about me as a person, but as a representative of Alix, I needed to make sure I always looked professional. Going to work with a bit of a sunburn made me look more like a child who'd been playing outside than an adult, so using makeup to keep the red to a minimum was necessary.

I needed to go shopping, I thought as I smoothed down my sundress. Back home, I'd always dressed comfortably, which for me had usually meant jeans with a variety of t-shirts and sweatshirts, often hand-me-downs from one brother or another. In college, I'd scoured thrift stores for slacks and blouses, and those had serviced me well in my previous jobs. Now, however, it was far too warm for pants and I certainly wouldn't wear shorts, but I'd never fancied capris, which meant I'd be wearing dresses or skirts. I'd give Alix no cause to be ashamed of my appearance.

I tugged at the dress, wishing it was a bit longer. If I remembered to bend at my knees instead of the waist, I should keep from embarrassing myself. Alix and I had developed a tentative truce at the moment, and I didn't want anything to spoil that, especially me accidentally flashing him a peek of my white cotton panties.

WHEN I ARRIVED at the studio, he was already there, tossing pillows and blankets into different piles, then frowning and doing it again. He glanced up as I set his coffee on the table next to his laptop, but didn't say anything. I didn't take his reticence personally. My observations over the past week had shown me that he didn't talk much in general, at least not when he was working. Direct questions with a point were answered, but personal inquiries rarely received answers, though he was warm enough when he gave those few answers to make me think that it was more about where his thoughts were when I asked than it was about him trying to keep his distance.

I took my coffee back to my office, already thinking about today's tasks. Ms. Holloman had asked me to send her a report of everything I'd done at the end of my first week, so that was my top priority. If I could land this job on a permanent basis, it'd go a long way to making me feel like I had enough job security to renew my lease. It'd also get Mam and Da off me about coming home.

"*This* is home," I reminded myself softly as I settled in my chair.

I took my time with my report, wanting to be thorough enough that Ms. Holloman could see that I was necessary, but not so detailed that I sounded like I was bragging. It was a fine line to walk, that was certain.

With that out of the way, I moved to Alix's email, weeding out the junk, the proposals no reputable artist – or decent person in general – would accept. Like an offer to star in an adult movie titled *Sorority House Humping III*.

When it was almost time for lunch, I called over to the Indian restaurant on the list of take-out places I found in the desk and put in an order for delivery. Less than twenty minutes later, I walked back through the studio and called over to Alix that I had lunch.

"Thai?" he asked as he came into the office.

"Indian." I gestured to the cartons on the desk. "Lamb curry, chicken makhai, chana masala, and shrimp biryani. Take your pick."

"Do you have a preference?"

I looked up, surprised at his question. "Not really."

I watched as he picked up one of the cartons, then

leaned on the desk next to me. The previous times I'd ordered lunch for us, he'd taken his back out to the studio to work while he ate. Today, though, he stayed.

Stayed and glowered at the lamb curry like it had personally insulted him.

I picked up the chana masala and took a few bites, but he still didn't say anything. Coming from a huge family, I liked the relative quiet I found here, but now, with neither one of us speaking...it didn't take long for it to make me feel awkward enough to break the silence.

"Is something wrong?"

He raised his head, those gray eyes not revealing anything below the surface. "Pardon?"

I gave him a partial smile. "You're looking at that food like it did you wrong."

He raised an eyebrow, but a corner of his mouth tipped up. I'd seen him with polite, professional smiles, but this one had some good-natured humor to it. "My parents and I spent a summer touring the UK when I was fourteen. Aside from taking pictures when I was there, the accents were my favorite part."

"As long as you don't go asking me to say anything about a pot o' gold or a certain sugary cereal, you can listen all you want."

The words popped out before I could decide if they were appropriate or not. Then he laughed, and I decided that there was something to be said for a relaxed work environment. The sound rolled over me, liquid heat that warmed me to the core.

"Thank you," he said. "I needed a good laugh."

"I do what I can." I took a couple more bites and waited for him to do the same before asking, "Is something bothering you?"

He frowned again and set down the carton, folding his arms across his chest. "That is the question, isn't it? Why do I bother?"

I tilted my head. "Have I missed some American idiom I've yet to learn?"

He shook his head. "I've been having issues with my work for a while now. I'll come up with a good idea, and I'll try it out, and maybe the first couple pictures will be okay, but then..." He sighed. "I can't think of how to describe it. I'm not good with words. That's my cousin Erik's forté. I just take pictures."

"I don't think there's anything *just* about the pictures you take."

"Thank you, Sine." He ran his hand through his hair. "I might've agreed with you at some point in the past, but now...I don't know why I'm even trying anymore."

I glanced toward the office door as something occurred to me. "I didn't see Giselle out there."

Alix pushed off the desk and began to pace, a sort of wild, restless energy buzzing around him. "That's because she sent me a text to say that she'd been offered a more lucrative job with a higher profile release. Since I said I didn't know what the hell I wanted to do, I told her to take it."

"That's a breach of contract, isn't it?"

He shook his head. "Not really, since it was my decision not to press it. Besides, I couldn't really blame her. My newest *inspiration* wasn't doing shit."

I considered him, worried at the lack of confidence showing in his eyes. "Maybe the idea was right, but the model was wrong."

I had a mouthful of food when he slowly turned at looked at me, an unreadable expression on his face. *Shite.* That hadn't been the nicest thing to say. I wasn't trying to be mean, and it really wasn't anything against Giselle.

I swallowed and scrambled to undo what I'd done. "I didn't mean it like–"

"You're right," he cut me off. His eyes were strangely bright. "I had the wrong person."

"Giselle is beautiful," I stammered. "And there are hundreds of other beautiful models out there. All of them just as professional as Giselle and I'm sure she'd understand that you'd be needing a different look. It's nothing against her, you see–"

He was smiling again, and I knew it was because my accent had gotten thicker. Or, at least, that's what I thought he was smiling about. Then he said five words that told me I had *no idea* what was happening.

"*You* can be my model."

6

SINE

I laughed as I waited for Alix's self-control to break and join in. Because it had to be a joke. While I knew my build might be good for modeling sportswear or children's clothes, I was at least eight inches too short for any photographer to look my way.

But he wasn't laughing or even cracking a smile now. All he was doing was looking at me with those eyes. That steady gray gaze that seemed to be waiting for me to realize that he was serious.

Fuck.

He *was* serious.

The laugh died in my throat even as my pulse raced. This wasn't possible. I had to be reading him wrong. Or maybe he was one of those total pricks who got off on cruel jokes. Because there was no way he meant that he wanted *me* to be a model.

I liked to think I had a fair grasp on my qualities, mentally and physically. I didn't think I was ugly, but I knew the difference between cute and beautiful. And I knew that strength and independence wasn't what most men found attractive. They definitely didn't want pseudo-sexy pictures of pint-sized tomboys.

Short girls were supposed to play up their curves or show a lot of skin. Or both. Tall ones who were slender showed off their long legs and the fact that they didn't always need to wear a bra. Slinky dresses with high hemlines and low necklines came in all sizes. Makeup. Feminine haircuts. High heels. Jewelry. Maybe a sexy tattoo.

Everything women did was supposed to express our sexuality, make us sensual. We were supposed to be attractive, even when downplaying the physical. And the girls who didn't follow those rules, regardless of how they looked, were somehow less. Dismissed by the majority.

I could own my intelligence, my strength, who I was. But that didn't mean I was sexy, no matter how much the media liked to say that confidence was sexy. The two guys I'd slept with hadn't seen me that way. There was no chance that after a week, a man like Alix would see what they hadn't.

"You made your point," I said finally. "I don't know enough about photography or modeling to make any suggestions."

"That's not what I said." He took a step toward me, his gaze moving slowly down my body.

I swallowed hard and tried to ignore the heat seeping across my skin. I'd never had anyone look at me like that before. Like they could see every flaw and imperfection, but that it only made me more interesting instead of less desirable.

"You were right," he repeated as his eyes met mine, held them. "I thought I was trying a different approach, but all I'd done was change props. The subject stayed the same, and that was a problem. I don't need someone who looks like Giselle."

I gave what I hoped was a self-deprecating smile. "Well, I definitely fit *that* description."

His expression changed, and for the first time since I'd come to work for him, I felt like he was seeing me. *Really* seeing me, not just acknowledging my presence. A genuine smile curved his mouth, making my stomach squirm in a way that wasn't appropriate for our employer-employee relationship.

"Different isn't always a bad thing, Sine."

I shrugged, unable to read what he was thinking. "It might not be bad, but it certainly is a risk, and one I don't understand you wanting to take. There's no logical reason you're asking me to model for you."

"I've been photographing Giselle for almost two weeks now," he said. "And before her, there were Lorna, Madison, Nessa, dozens over the past ten years. They all had different coloring and body types, and all had been modeling for at least a year or two. They sat where I wanted them to sit, moved, turned, posed. Complete professionals."

I nodded even though I had absolutely no idea where this conversation was going.

"I've sold probably hundreds of photographs of models like Giselle, but somewhere along the way, they all started to look alike." He closed the rest of the distance between us until I had to tip my head back to see his face. "I need someone new, someone different."

Different. That was me for certain.

"Unless," he paused, considering for a moment before going on, "you're not up for the challenge."

My eyes narrowed, and that part of me that had always pushed me to keep up with guys who were older and bigger flared up. "I have six brothers who spent most of my childhood telling me I was too young or too small to do what they were doing. There's no challenge I'm not up to beating."

Alix's eyes gleamed. "Glad to hear it. I'll go get things set up. Finish your lunch and then come out so I can give you your costume to change into."

He walked out of the office, leaving me staring at him and wondering what in the hell I'd just gotten myself into. I hadn't been thinking about actually *doing* it. I'd just never been able to back down when someone said I couldn't do something. Mam had always told me that taking a dare would land me in trouble someday. I knew for a fact she hadn't foreseen that the trouble in question would be me posing for erotic photographs.

Neither had I, but a part of me wanted to know if I could see what he saw in me. Another part was running through all the possible arguments I could use to get out of what was going to be an incredibly awkward situation.

7

ALIX

I hadn't told Jean yet, but I was actually grateful she'd hired an assistant.

No, that wasn't entirely accurate. I was grateful she'd hired *Sine*.

By the middle of the first week, Sine had shown a dedicated work ethic, as well as a knack for organization that went well beyond my own more haphazard system. She went above and beyond. And I supposed that was why I'd started noticing her. Or maybe I'd seen her from moment one, but just hadn't acknowledged it.

When I didn't have music on, I could hear her moving around in the office, talking quietly in that lilting Irish voice of hers. I generally couldn't make out specific words, but it was pleasant. Something about it eased the tension I'd been carrying at the base of my skull.

We hadn't really talked much before, not beyond work basics, but when I'd seen her come in today, I hadn't been able to take my eyes off her. She was wearing a sundress, a pale green that suited her coloring, but something about it didn't quite sit right with me. It wasn't until she disappeared into the office that I realized what it was. For the first time since I met her, she didn't seem quite comfortable in her own skin.

Giselle's text about quitting had interrupted my thoughts, so by the time Sine came back out to get out food from the delivery boy, all that tension was back. The conversation that followed had surprised me, both because it'd been completely unplanned, and because of how much I enjoyed it.

I was a quiet person by nature, not one to make idle conversation. Even as a Dom, I didn't use excessive words, but with Sine, they'd come easily. I'd found myself looking at her. Studying the lines of her face, the freckles across her nose and cheeks. The shade of her eyes was extraordinary, and I started wondering in which ways it would shift with different colors accenting it.

It wasn't until she made the comment about how the problem might have been with Giselle that it hit me.

She was right. I'd been focusing so hard on the external, on the props, that I hadn't considered that a new inspiration might need a new model. Not just new in the sense of someone I hadn't worked with before, but rather new to the whole concept of modeling.

I had to admit, I was surprised at her response. Most women would've jumped at the chance to become a model. She wasn't just being modest either. I could see it on her face, in her eyes. She honestly didn't see why I'd want her to pose for me. Okay, so she didn't have the flashy beauty like Giselle, but she was still striking.

And then I'd realized what I hadn't before. How she'd looked pretty in her sundress, but not comfortable. Thinking I was joking when I said I wanted her to model. Her usual attire that was so different from what most of the women around me wore.

She honestly didn't see her allure. She didn't think she was sexy.

Which somehow made me want to photograph her even more. I now realized that was what my concept had been missing. The juxtaposition of innocence and sensuality. The various bondage techniques I'd been trying on Giselle all week could easily be adapted for Sine's different body type.

Before we did anything, I needed to make sure she knew that no matter how erotic the photos I took were, I didn't cross the line with my models. It wasn't as hard as most people would think. I could appreciate beauty without sexual attraction, especially when I was behind my camera. I always kept sex and art separate, so I was confident I could keep things professional.

I heard her footsteps before she spoke. "I won't be insulted if you've realized it's a mistake for me to...*model*." The word came out flat, like she couldn't quite believe she was saying it.

I glanced over at her, noted how she nervously fidgeted with the hem of her dress, then smiled. "Actually,

I was just out here working through what I wanted to do first."

She frowned, clearly skeptical, but she didn't argue, so that was good. I tossed the pillows aside and smoothed out a plain black blanket. It was thick and soft so it wouldn't be uncomfortable for her to lay on for the next couple hours. When I straightened and turned to face her, I found her watching me. A surprising flush of heat went through me, and I reminded my treacherous libido that this was work only.

"I'll not be taking my clothes off," she said firmly, folding her arms over her stomach, the gesture pushing her pert breasts into cleavage that I had to force myself to ignore.

I shook my head. "When you were going through things, did you happen to read one of the modeling contracts? I don't do nudity."

She raised an eyebrow.

"Erotic, yes," I said. "Sexual. Sensual. Yes and yes. Sometimes close to nudity, okay, but never all the way there. And it's all tastefully done."

"I still don't understand why you want me to do this," Sine said.

"Chickening out?" I told myself that the good-natured teasing was to put her at ease, not to provoke her, but I knew that was a lie. If I worded things a different way, she probably would take the out, but if I pushed that same button this time that I had before, she'd push back.

She glared at me. "I don't *chicken out*."

"Then humor me." I gave her my most charming grin. "I promise to be completely professional."

I watched as she thought it over but didn't say anything. It had to be her choice. Nervous was okay, but I never wanted a woman to feel pressured into anything by me. I could be intense, I knew, and sometimes intimidated people, even if I didn't intend it. If this was going to work, she had to trust me.

"What about my other responsibilities? I need a steady job."

"You'll have a separate contract for modeling," I promised. "And a long-term one as my assistant." When she hesitated, I added, "I can work this on a per session basis, so there's no obligation to continue, but you'll get paid a lump sum at the end of each week. How does that sound?"

Her hands curled into fists, flexed, uncurled.

"I'll work with you today," she said finally. "But I make no promises beyond that."

"Understood."

I glanced toward the wardrobe where I kept the costumes I'd selected for this shoot. None of them would work for Sine. Giselle was half a foot taller.

"What are you wearing under your dress?" Her eyes widened, and I raised my hands in a *wait* gesture. "No nudity, but yes, you'll need to show some skin. It's part of the design I want to do. But nothing I have will fit you."

A blush stained her cheeks almost immediately as she

understood that I'd looked at her body close enough to know something about her measurements.

"What are you wearing?" I repeated the question and told myself that I only wanted to know to determine what I'd be able to do. It had nothing to do with the way my stomach tightened at the thought of filmy lace barely covering...

"Nothing special," she said, eyes sliding away from me. "Cotton. Green."

My cock twitched. Shit. That shouldn't have been so hot.

I took a slow breath and reminded myself that this was work. Nothing more.

I nodded and told myself I was ready. "All right. Let me see."

8

SINE

I changed my mind, Mr. Wexler. I'm sorry. I acted a fool, taking that challenge seriously. I don't think this is appropriate.

Every possible excuse raced through my mind, some so ridiculous that they were laughable, but plenty would have worked. I'd only known Alix for a week, but I knew he'd let it go if I asked. And a part of me desperately wanted to ask because this was certainly far out of my comfort zone.

But another, louder, part wanted to give it a try. It was this side of me that had always pushed me to do the crazy things. Climbing into the church rafters during Mass. Running into the pasture and scaring the sheep. Throwing a mud pie at Mr. Fitzpatrick when he was hitting his dog. Taking out goalie Liam O'Leary's feet during a football match because he'd called Donald a foul name.

None of those had been good ideas, and I was fairly certain that this one ranked up there as one of the dumbest, but when Alix asked if I was chickening out, I knew I couldn't back down.

I took a slow breath as I lowered my zipper. Every inch of my skin felt like it was on fire. I'd taken my clothes off in front of guys before, but those times had been rushed, and they'd been taking off their own too, not standing in front of me fully clothed, watching. I let the dress drop, then stepped out of it. Neither Alix nor I said anything as I picked it up and hung it on a nearby hook.

His gaze ran down my body and back up again as I tried not to fidget. My bra and panties matched, but they were exactly what I'd told him. Pale green cotton. Nothing special. Certainly not like the finery to which he was accustomed.

"We'll start simple," he said, looking away from me. He gestured toward the floor where he'd spread a blanket. "Lie down."

Hoping he couldn't hear my heart thudding against my ribcage, I slipped my shoes off and went over to the blanket. I sat down, then realized that I didn't know how he wanted me to lay. A professional model certainly would've known what to do, but all I could do was sit there mutely and try to decide if I should lie on my back, my side, or my stomach.

"Sine." His voice was surprisingly gentle. "Relax. I promise, this won't hurt a bit."

I looked up to see him smiling at me. My stomach did a little flip and I frowned. His expression immediately sobered, misunderstanding the reason for my change in expression. I didn't intend to correct him, however. It was embarrassing enough that I'd had a flash of attraction. I didn't want to explain it.

"You don't have to do this."

This was it. My out. He wouldn't tease me about it, and I knew he wouldn't hold it against me either. But I would. I'd know that I had backed off from this when I'd never backed away from anything.

"How do you want me?"

Heat flooded my face as I realized how my question sounded, but I refused to take it back.

Alix's eyes darkened for a moment, then cleared. "On your back."

"You're the boss," I said as I laid down, telling myself that I didn't look as awkward as I felt.

"Arms above your head."

I complied, letting out another breath. Maybe this wasn't as awful as all that. He didn't expect me to come up with ideas of my own. All I had to do was follow his directions. Normally, I'd balk at being told what to do, but I was so far out of my depth here that it actually eased my nerves rather than aggravating them.

"I'm going to restrain your wrists now."

I kept my eyes on the ceiling, but couldn't stop the shiver that ran over me as his fingertips brushed my skin. I felt something against my wrists, but not metal handcuffs as I'd anticipated. Cloth. Something soft and cool. Silk most likely. It took only a minute or two, and then he was walking back to where he'd set up his camera.

Music was playing in the background, so we weren't in total silence, but I had to bite my bottom lip to keep from chattering just to ease the nerves that had reappeared the moment he went behind his camera.

"Relax."

I raised an eyebrow. "Would you like to take my place and see how well you're able to relax?"

He laughed, and it wasn't sort of polite laugh one gave to acknowledge something intended to be amusing. He actually thought my comment was funny.

"Where's your favorite place to go?"

"What do you mean?"

"If you could go anywhere for one day to relax, where would you go?"

"The sea," I answered automatically. "Not the coast here, but back in Ireland. The smell of salt on the air. The crash of water against the rocks."

I wasn't even aware that my muscles were no longer tense until I heard the faint clicking of the camera. I kept going, describing the place I'd once considered my refuge. I didn't stop until he came over to me again.

Instead of untying my wrists, he began to wrap my forearms, the new position putting some strain on my shoulders. Not enough that it was painful, but it was definitely new and not exactly comfortable...but oddly *comforting*.

"If any of this hurts you, just tell me."

I nodded, more aware of his touch than his words. His fingers were strong, but not rough. The way he wrapped the silk around my arms from wrist to elbow was quick, but not sloppy. I couldn't see it, but I could feel how each scarf rested against my skin.

"We'll start with some pictures with you like this," he said, his voice low as his fingers brushed through my hair. He twisted and adjusted my curls, everything about him clinical, professional. "And then we'll move you around a bit, see what else strikes me. How does that sound?"

I nodded. I could do that.

I WASN'T AN IMPULSIVE PERSON. I thought things through, planned. It was why I'd graduated at the top of my class, how I'd done so well in college, why I was good at my job. It was also how I managed to convince my parents that I wouldn't end up being a prostitute in the Big Apple because I was in over my head.

I told my college roommate that once, and she laughed like I was joking, but that really happened. Mam had been convinced that I wouldn't be able to handle living on my own, especially not in New York City. Only my brother Donald had supported me from moment one. Being gay in a Catholic family came with its own set of difficulties. I'd stuck by him from moment one, and he'd done the same for me.

I wondered if he'd support me now.

Alix had stuck to his word about no nudity, and he'd been nothing but professional yesterday, but I doubted any of that would make my family comfortable with what I'd done. I was all about women being empowered to make their own choices about their bodies, so I didn't believe I'd done anything wrong, but that didn't mean I liked the idea of telling my parents – or my overprotective brothers – that I stripped down to my underthings, let a man tie my arms up, and then take pictures for the world to see.

And I for certain wouldn't be telling them that a part of me had enjoyed it.

I was already regretting posing for him before I even gotten home last night, and the anxious thoughts had kept me tossing and turning. I'd only gotten through today because I'd kept busy. Cooking. Cleaning. Spending a couple hours on Skype, first with Mam and then with Donald. Now, all that was done, and even a long bath hadn't been enough to stop my brain from going over all the possible ways one poor decision could seriously fuck up my life.

How was I ever going to face Alix again? Sure, all the essential bits had been as covered as they would've been in a bikini – more than some – but it had felt different. Alix had been a complete gentleman, giving instructions, and only touching when necessary, but I'd still been so aware of him that by the time the session had ended, my hands had been shaking.

He'd excused himself to the darkroom to give me privacy to get dressed, and I'd appreciated it, but a part of me still wondered if he'd realized how strange it would be to see each other on Monday. Though, I supposed it was possible that he was accustomed to this sort of thing. Photograph a woman in something revealing, then talk to her like he hadn't seen anything intimate.

But it hadn't been *intimate*, I reminded myself. We'd shared nothing precious, done nothing shameful.

I sighed as I rummaged through the kitchen, trying to find something to distract me. The only alcohol in my apartment was whiskey from back home, but I didn't think that would be a wise idea. I could hold my own better than one would think for someone my size, but I didn't fancy dealing with a hangover if I let myself drink enough to forget. Ice cream would've been my preference, but I didn't have any of that. Money had been tight since my former roommate moved back to Nashville three months ago, leaving me with the full cost of rent.

The money from yesterday's photo shoot was more needed than I wanted to admit. I couldn't go back and change things, so there wasn't much point in going on about it, but I could be smarter in the future. I'd go in on Monday and tell Alix that while I appreciated the opportunity, I'd be taking payment for one session and going back to my original job as his assistant.

I found a container of frozen grapes and smiled. Marcia, my former roommate, had turned me on to those during a brown-out two summers ago. Not ice cream, but still a treat.

I popped one into my mouth, grabbed a bottle of water, and curled up in my favorite chair. I was ten minutes into my favorite episode of Britain's most famous science fiction series when someone knocked at my door.

I frowned as I paused the show and pushed myself up out of my chair. At least three times a month, some delivery person came to my door instead of going up one more floor to the Del Rio place.

Except when I looked out, it wasn't a delivery. It was Alix.

I flipped both the deadbolts and unchained the door, opening it before I remembered that I was wearing my most comfortable – and therefore my most worn – pajamas. The shorts weren't those cute little ones that most girls wore, but rather a pair from my high school football – soccer in America – league, sporting our colors of purple and white. My shirt had been a hand-me-down from my oldest brother, Patrick, when he'd moved out. He wasn't the biggest of my brothers but big enough that the shirt almost covered my shorts, and the neck often slid off my shoulder.

Alix didn't comment on my outfit and I motioned for him to come inside. I closed the door, crossing my arms as I turned to face him. My pulse began to race even as my stomach tied itself in knots. His expression was serious, his eyes stormy, and I didn't know what had happened to make him this way. Whatever it was, I knew he wasn't here to borrow a cup of sugar.

"The pictures came out amazing," he said, pacing to the lone window before turning to come back toward me.

"They were exactly what I imagined. The color and lighting and..." His eyes met mine. "You were perfect."

I supposed now was as good a time as any to tell him that I'd decided those would be the only photos he'd get to take. But even as I opened my mouth, he was talking again.

"We need to do more. I have a whole range of ideas for a series. And if you're worried about people recognizing you, I can make it work without showing your face, or I'll give you a mask."

A series? Dammit. He wanted to *display* the pictures. I was an idiot for thinking otherwise. I hadn't even considered what it would mean to have people looking at them. Stupid, I knew, but entirely on me.

"You have no idea how long I'd been looking for someone to make things come alive again." He was suddenly directly in front of me, the faint scent of tea tree oil soap surrounding me. "So, what do say, Sine?"

I was having trouble breathing, much less thinking. I shouldn't do it. I had dozens of reasons why it was a bad idea. For one thing, I wasn't a model. "Now that you've found what you want to do, you should look for a real model to complete the series." My nails dug into my forearms as I resisted the urge to touch him. Whatever energy between us at the studio was nothing compared to what I felt weaving between us now.

"A real model?" he echoed my words.

I sighed. "You have to know that no man will want to look at a series of photographs of me trying to be sexy."

Something strange passed across his eyes, and then his

hands were on my elbows, yanking me toward him even as he bent his head to take my mouth.

I could have stopped him, pushed him away, and I knew he would have respected it. But I didn't. I let his lips come down hard on mine, heat and electricity racing across my nerves the moment we touched. I leaned into him, let his tongue part my lips, glide across mine.

He groaned, hands sliding up my arms, and then down my back, freeing me to wrap my arms around his neck. I forgot that he was my boss. Forgot that I didn't look like the women he'd had in the past or the ones he'd have in the future.

His hands moved lower, cupping my ass as he lifted me. I wrapped my legs around his waist, digging my fingers into his hair. He bit my bottom lip, then soothed the sting with his tongue.

"Fuck, Sine," he breathed as he rested his forehead against mine. "I want you."

Bad idea.

Really bad idea.

"First door on the right." My voice was breathless.

So...bad idea it was.

I kissed along his jaw as he carried me the short distance to my bedroom. It was tiny, barely large enough for my double bed, so it took only two steps once through the doorway for Alix to reach it. He set me down, fingers catching the bottom of my shirt. He paused before he pulled it off completely, the question written on his face. I nodded.

The shirt landed somewhere on the floor, and my shorts followed, leaving me completely naked...and suddenly self-conscious. I began to cover myself, then stopped at the sharp command.

"Stop."

My eyes darted up to his, and the desire that had darkened them threw away any doubt I had about him wanting this.

He cupped my chin, ran his thumb along my bottom lip. "Do you trust me?"

I nodded.

"I want–" He hesitated, then ran his fingers through my hair, touched my cheek. There was something strange about it, almost uncertain.

"Tell me."

"I want to tie you up."

That should have been the sort of statement that made me tell him to leave, but it wasn't shocking. Not really.

"Like you did yesterday." It wasn't a question.

He slid his hand down to move his thumb over my nipple. I shivered.

"Yes, like yesterday. Except this time, I'll definitely be touching. And a whole lot more." His voice was low. "But only if you want me."

I held my hands out in front of me, forearms together. "I don't have any ribbons, but use what you will."

Judging by the look on his face, he hadn't expected me to say that. "Have you done anything like this before?"

"You mean aside from yesterday?" I smiled at him. "No."

If anything, his eyes darkened even more. "You're not a–"

I shook my head. "No. But I am getting a wee bit chilly," I teased.

He chuckled, and the sound heated me. "Lie back. Arms above your head."

I did as he asked, stretching out on my bed as he went over to the robe hanging on the back of my door and pulled off the belt.

"Are you going to take off your clothes?"

He paused, another of those strange expressions passing across his face. He tossed the belt next to me, then pulled his shirt over his head, revealing a firm, sculpted torso.

Fuck.

He was his own work of art.

I watched him as he came over and wrapped the robe's belt around my forearms. The short-sleeved shirts he'd worn in the studio hadn't done him justice. As he shifted, I saw a tattoo covering the top half of his back, a bird of some sort, the wings across his shoulder blades.

"Eagle?" I asked as he moved around to stand near my feet.

"Phoenix." He ran his fingers up my calf. "You really have no idea how sexy you look like this, do you?"

My heart gave a funny thump. He'd been intense yesterday behind the camera, but this was something else. "I bet you say that to all the girls you tie up," I teased.

He smiled. "Not at all."

Before I could try to figure out what he meant by that, he was kicking his pants aside, and I was...distracted. The half-dozen darkened fumblings I'd had in college hadn't left much time or light for me to see much, but I had no doubt that neither of my exes could measure up to Alix Wexler – combined.

"Shit," Alix muttered.

It was only then that I realized he was holding something in his hands.

"Damn condom tore." He tossed it into the trash. "I only had one." He smiled at me. "Guess we'll have to stick to another kind of fun."

I shook my head. If we didn't do this now, I doubted we ever would. And I wanted it. Wanted him. "I'm on the pill, and I haven't been with anyone in a couple years."

He studied me for a moment, and I could see him weighing the pros and cons. The moment I saw him surrender to his desire, my stomach twisted. "I get tested regularly. I'm clean." He kneeled on the bed, hands resting on my ankles. "Are you sure?"

"Come on now, you're not going to be leaving a lass all tied up with nowhere to go, are you?" I purposefully thickened my accent, grinning up at him.

He smiled back, leaning down to take my nipple between his lips. I gasped, arching up against him, surprised at the rough suction.

"Too much?" he asked, glancing up at me.

"No," I breathed. "More."

Guys usually treated me like I was going to break, but Alix didn't seem to have that problem. His thumb stroked over my clit, the pressure hard enough to make me jerk. Teeth worried at my nipple, sharp bites of pain that didn't cancel out the pleasure from his mouth and his hand. He slid a finger inside, and my head fell back, eyes closed.

"Look at me, Sine."

I squirmed, hips moving as his finger and thumb continued to work between my legs. My hands opened and closed over my head, the need to touch, to hold, frustrated me more than I thought possible.

"Sine."

He didn't shout, but the authority in his voice made me open my eyes. I gasped as a second finger pushed inside, but as soon as my eyelids started fluttering...

"Don't."

I looked at him, saw the dark hair fall across his forehead, and my fingers itched to push it back.

"I want to touch you," I confessed, my voice close to begging. "Please, Alix."

He shook his head, eyes on my face as he bent his head, flicked his tongue against my nipple. He twisted his fingers, sending a new rush of sensations through me.

"Don't close your eyes," he cautioned. "I want you watching me as I make you come on my fingers."

Sex with my two previous partners hadn't been entirely unpleasant, but I'd had to use my own fingers to make sure

I finished. If the pressure building in my belly was any indication, I wouldn't need to do that tonight.

"I know you don't believe you're desirable," he said quietly. "But you are, Sine. I desire you. I *see* you."

His thumb circled my clit faster, drawing out gasps and moans as he pushed me closer to the edge.

"You can trust me," he continued. "Let me show you how good it can be. Do you want that?"

I nodded, every muscle in my body tensing, coiling in anticipation. I bit my lower lip, vaguely remembering how thin my walls were. Then his mouth was on my breast again, and I came, hard enough to make him swear as my pussy clamped down on his fingers.

I was still breathing hard when he moved over me. I'd known he was much bigger than me, but I hadn't really felt it until now. He balanced on his elbows, his body hovering over mine, close enough that I could feel the heat radiating off his skin. For a long moment, we stayed like that, and then his mouth was on mine again. He kissed me hard and deep, lowering his body until I felt the tip of him pushing against me. I cried out as he eased his way inside, but he swallowed the sound.

Our bodies shouldn't have fit together, shouldn't have been able to move this way. He was so big all over, he could crush me, tear me in half, but he didn't. Even as he moved inside me, filling me almost to the point of pain, I could feel the restraint, the sheer magnitude of the power he held back.

Each stroke made me struggle against my restraints,

desperate to have some form of control, some outlet for everything building inside me. All I could do was take it, absorb it, until it all became too much and I exploded.

Even through the white-hot pleasure of my climax, I felt him jerk against me, bury himself deep. And then he was coming too, groaning out my name, and I knew that no matter what we said or intended, things would never be the same.

9

ALIX

I kept going over things in my head, trying to figure out when I'd changed from wanting Sine to continue modeling for me to simply wanting *her*. She was nothing like the women I usually went for. I'd always preferred slender builds, but Sine was the definition of petite. When I picked her up the other night and carried her to her bedroom, I realized just how small she was. For a moment, when I'd been above her, I had the sudden urge to tell her that I'd protect her, keep her safe. That I'd never let anyone hurt her. Not even me. Not even if I had to walk away.

But that thought hadn't been enough to stop me from sinking into her, from finding pleasure in her body.

It hadn't been until I'd untied her and started rubbing her arms and hands to get the circulation flowing properly that I'd realized just how stupid I'd been. She was my assistant and my model, not some nameless Sub I met at a club. And while Sine might not have been a virgin, she definitely wasn't experienced, especially not in bondage. Having sex with her could ruin everything.

I'd always vowed I'd never be the sort of sleazy photographer who'd seduce his models, and until Saturday night, I'd kept that promise.

I hadn't lingered, but I hadn't exactly snuck out either. I cleaned myself up in her tiny bathroom before letting her know I'd see myself out. She hadn't seemed upset when she'd gone to take a shower, but I'd been too cowardly to wait around to make sure she was okay. Now, I was kicking myself for that.

What if she didn't come in today? She would be well within her rights to file a harassment claim, or even something worse if she felt like I'd pressured her into sex. I could lose her as an assistant and as a model, and that would be the very least of the consequences my rash actions could have. It wasn't outside the realm of possibility that she could sue me, drag my name through the mud. And it'd be all my fault.

When Jean had told me to behave myself with Sine, she hadn't meant this, but if she found out what happened, she'd kick me to the curb. She'd always been so proud that I wasn't one of those asshole artists who kept needing to be bailed out of jail. And while my sexual preferences for BDSM weren't public knowledge, I didn't try to hide my membership at Gilded Cage either. I was neither a recluse nor a partier, neither a serial romancer or a life-long bachelor. I didn't see myself in the tabloids, and I liked it that way.

While I waited to see if Sine would show up, I brought out the photos from our session Friday night and spread them out on the floor so I could see them in relation to each other. I was kneeling next to a particularly evocative one when I heard the door open. I made myself count to ten before raising my head, not wanting to appear too eager to see her. I didn't want her to get the wrong idea.

"I didn't realize you'd taken so many of them."

She wasn't looking at me, but rather at the pictures, giving me the opportunity to study her without being obvious about it. She didn't look any different than she had on Friday, except she was back to a pair of dress slacks and a nice blouse rather than her sundress.

"I'll let you know if I need you to answer any emails personally," she said as she turned to go. "Your coffee's on the table."

"Do you have anything planned for this afternoon?" I sat back on my heels and ignored the voice in the back of my head telling me this was an imprudent idea. To say the least.

"Nothing specific." Her eyes met mine for a moment, her cheeks growing pink before she glanced away, focusing instead on the cup she held in her hands.

"I'd like you to model for me again." I rose to my feet but went for my coffee instead of going to her like my body wanted to.

In the silence that followed, a hundred thoughts ran

through my mind, everything from her stomping out in a huff, to her calling the cops, to her taking that to mean I wanted her in my bed. The memory of what she felt like made my stomach tighten, but I knew it couldn't happen again. Once could be written off as an impulsive mistake. Twice...that would be the start of a pattern I didn't want.

"I would be open to that," she said slowly, her finger tracing around the lid of her cup. "But we need to have some rules in place."

I nodded, took a long gulp of my iced cafe latte before speaking. "That's a good idea. Did you have anything specific in mind?"

"Two."

I blinked. If she had two rules ready so quickly, it meant she'd already been thinking about this. I was surprised but not displeased.

"It has to stay professional between us," she said, her voice steady. "What happened the other night, it can't happen again. I'm your assistant, and you're my boss. A model and photographer. Nothing more."

I nodded, relieved that she wasn't going to blow things up because of a moment of shared weakness. "I want the same thing."

"And no nudity," she said, eyes darting up to my face again. "It doesn't matter that you've already seen..." She lifted her chin. "I won't be doing anything like that."

"Agreed."

She nodded once and then turned away. "I'll let you

know when I order lunch, and we can get started after that."

I couldn't have hoped for a better outcome, I thought as I watched her disappear into her office. No awkward silences or wondering what the other one was thinking. No worries that she'd gotten the wrong idea, no demands or threats of legal action. It should have been everything I could have wanted.

Then why did the thought of touching her again after lunch make me feel elated? That I'd have a reason to feel her soft skin against my palms. That every single idea I had for today's session morphed into what it would be like to tie her up, pose her, not for photographs, but so that I could lose myself in her again.

She was right to want this to stay professional, but I wasn't so sure of my own motives anymore.

10

SINE

I'd always been a bit in awe of artists, being able to picture things and then create them. Painters, sculptures, authors, photographers. Mam had a knack for making all manner of things with a needle and thread. Da was a genius with a knife for carving, and a couple of my brothers had the same skill. My sister won every baking contest she entered.

Me? I could organize and schedule. Some talent.

Alix...he could visualize things I couldn't even dream. I might not have understood what he saw in me, but I'd seen the photos he'd taken, and I couldn't deny that they were special. Though I knew that was more due to Alix's talent than me being his subject.

Which meant I was a part of his art in a way, and that made me see modeling for him in a whole new way.

None of that changed how his touch made my skin

hum or the fact that I couldn't stop thinking about what he felt like, smelled like. The things he made me feel.

Like safe.

I'd worn another set of matching bra and panties, these ones white cotton. It'd been a little easier to undress this time, but as I knelt on the blanket and waited for him to tie me up, the anticipation racing along my nerves was more intense than before.

He used leather this time, connecting my wrists to my ankles tight enough that I didn't have much in the way of mobility. It forced my back to arch, putting my breasts on display, which was made even more embarrassing by the fact that my nipples were hard little points, easily visible. And I couldn't even blame it on temperature because the lights were hot enough to make me appreciate not having to wear more clothes.

When he finished, he walked around in front of me, and I tilted my head back so I could see his face. He leaned down and rested his hand on the side of my face. His thumb moved across my lower lip, and it took all my self-control not to lick it.

Dammit.

This was going to be harder than I thought.

BY THE TIME I got home, my skin felt like it was on too tight, my body flushed. I felt antsy, like I couldn't quite sit still. I paced as I waited for my dinner to heat up, but even as I ate, I fidgeted. Fingernails tapping against the table. Chopsticks stabbing into the reheated rice.

I just couldn't relax.

I must have tossed and turned for an hour before I accepted the fact that I wouldn't get any sleep unless I did something else to relax.

It was far too easy to recall his face in my mind, see his strong jaw and those smoky eyes. Easy to pretend that the hand pushing up my t-shirt, and then sliding under my panties, was his. My own fingers were so much smaller than his, but I let my mind fill in the blanks, change the way I knew things were.

His lips made their way down my stomach, his fingers brushing over the thin red curls, then dipping between my folds. I gasped, arched my back. As his finger entered me, his thumb moved over my swollen clit, sending wave after wave of pleasure through me.

"You have no idea how beautiful you are, do you?" His voice was low, full of desire. "Come for me, Sine. Come, and then I'll taste you. I want my mouth on you, want to bring you pleasure. I want to bury my cock in your tight pussy, fuck you until neither of us can see straight."

The pressure on my clit was nearly unbearable, riding that thin line that only he seemed able to find. His free hand slid up to cover my breast, fingers rolling then twisting my nipple. Pleasure and pain blended together, and I writhed against his touch, wanting, needing...

I came with a shout, barely holding back his name. It was bad enough I'd been fantasizing about him and touching myself. Saying his name would make more of it than I wanted. He was attractive. Any straight woman or gay man could see that for themselves. It was no different than picturing another good-looking man. That's all there was to it. Nothing more.

All that existed between Alix and me was a business relationship that was a touch more complicated than most.

11

ALIX

I always thought of myself as the sort of person who owned their actions. If I did wrong, I didn't try to hide it. I accepted the consequences and tried to make better decisions.

Which was why I was feeling like shit for having taken things too far with Sine. And even worse for not being able to stop myself from thinking about her yesterday when my libido had gotten the better of me. When I'd gotten home, I had the shower so cold that I'd almost been shivering, but it hadn't done a thing to diminish my throbbing erection. I'd known that only one thing could do that, and I hadn't been able to hold back. It had been her face I'd seen as I wrapped my hand around my cock. Her voice I'd heard saying my name, heard moaning in pleasure.

And it had been her name I'd said when I'd reached my climax.

The guilt I'd felt when I was done hadn't stopped me

from dreaming about her. Or from thinking about her almost non-stop all morning when she was in the office. I had an all afternoon meeting with Jean to discuss my new line, so there'd be no modeling today, but as I worked on what I was going to tell Jean, Sine was in my head. Usually, when I had an idea, I saw around the model, but with this one, she was key.

Jean was waiting at our usual restaurant, already munching on her favorite appetizer. I barely sat down when our regular waiter brought over a bottle of Merlot. I wasn't much for day drinking, but Jean and I always indulged in some wine with our business lunches. I was especially grateful for that today. I needed something to help me relax. My cock would've preferred a whole other course of action, but sex with Sine was off the table.

And my word choice, of course, made me think of spreading Sine out *on* the table, and I was glad that the way I sat kept anyone from seeing that just the thought of her was enough to make me hard.

"You look tired," Jean observed. "I hope that's a good thing. I've had two gallery owners call me, wanting to schedule a showing for Alix Wexler's new line-up."

"I have one," I said and was pleased to see her relieved smile. "I tried a couple things and got inspired. I plan on talking to Sine tomorrow about signing the release papers."

Jean's eyes narrowed. "Sine? As in Sine McNiven? The nice Irish girl I hired to be the assistant you didn't want?"

I took a drink of my wine and then swiped a stuffed mushroom from Jean's plate. "You were right."

"Did you choke on those words?" Jean asked with an amused smile. "They have to be hard to swallow."

"Fine, fine." I shook my head, laughing. "Enjoy your moment." I slid a manila envelope across the table. "Then take a look at these."

She opened the envelope after the waiter took our orders, taking her time to really look at each of the dozen photos I carefully selected. It was Jean's usual practice. She needed to have an idea of what I wanted to do so she could sell it the best way.

"You had your assistant model for you." She started through the pictures a second time, shaking her head. "Didn't I tell you to behave yourself with her? She's twenty-three years old, Alix. What were you thinking?"

I frowned. "I was thinking that Sine's an adult who can make her own choices."

Jean put the photos back into the envelope. "If she decides you pressured her into taking those, you could end up in serious legal trouble."

"I made sure the lines were clear," I said, feeling like a little boy defending himself. "And I'm taking care of the legalities."

"Will the new line be as erotic as these?" Jean asked, her tone strangely disapproving.

She'd never asked that before, not like that. When Jean and I had first sat down more than a decade ago to discuss how our professional relationship was going to work, she told me that she'd never try to direct my art, that she would only market it as I created it.

"You've never had a problem with my subject matter in the past," I said mildly. "Why the change?"

Jean leaned forward. "She's not a model, Alix. She's a good kid."

"Is this where I'm supposed to promise that my intentions are pure and that I won't corrupt her?" I ran my finger around the rim of my glass.

"Could you promise any of that honestly?" Jean countered.

I considered her question. Were my intentions for Sine pure? Was I going to corrupt her if I followed through on my series idea?

I knew there were two ways to answer those questions, and they all depended on whether or not I could maintain the professional boundaries that Sine and I had set in place.

The series I wanted to do was more sexualized than these pictures. They would delve deeper into the life I kept private, and I knew I would have to expose that part of myself to Sine if I wanted her to trust me enough to do the series. Doing that would make it difficult to keep seeing her in a platonic way. If she was another model, it wouldn't have been a problem, but there was something about her...

I didn't believe there was anything wrong with my sexual preferences. I was of the belief that anything was permissible as long as it occurred between consenting adults. So, introducing Sine to my world wouldn't corrupt her, but I wasn't certain Jean would agree. And I certainly couldn't tell her that I knew Sine wasn't a virgin because the ensuing conversation about how, exactly, I'd come to learn that particular little tidbit wouldn't lead anywhere good.

"She inspired me," I said finally. "I've been...adrift for months. You know it. You've seen what I've tried to work with, but as soon as I started taking Sine's photos, it was like I could see everything."

Jean's eyebrows went up. "I've never heard you talk like this before."

"Because I've never met anyone like her before." I drained the last of my wine. "Sine is my muse. She's my inspiration, Jean. I can't explain it, but when I'm with her..."

I let my voice trail off before I said something I couldn't take back.

The expression on Jean's face, however, suggested that she didn't need words to see that inspiration wasn't all that Sine meant to me, no matter how much I was trying to deny it.

12

SINE

Since Alix hadn't said anything to me yesterday about wanting me to model for him again, I decided that going into work early this morning would be the best way to avoid an awkward conversation. If I was already working when he came in, I could control the conversation, or at least look busy while he talked. If I looked into his eyes and saw that, for some unknown reason, he still wanted me, I couldn't say I was confident in my ability to say no.

I told myself it was because he was good-looking, and that it was due to how he made me feel physically, but deep down I knew I was lying to myself with those excuses. I didn't have the ability to fully explain what it was about him that drew me in and made me lose focus, but I knew I needed to get ahold of it if I could ever make this work.

Which brought me back to wanting to be in the office by the time Alix arrived.

The moment I reached the studio door and found it unlocked, however, I realized my plan already had failed. As I walked inside, Alix pushed off the table he'd been leaning against and walked toward me.

"I figured that since you bring me coffee all the time, I'd return the favor." He raised his hands to show cups from the same bodega I'd purchased the two cups I held. "One can never have too much caffeine."

I nodded dumbly. He'd caught me off-guard, showing up early, offering me coffee. If it hadn't been for the fact that we'd already said no more sex, I might have thought he was trying to get me into bed again. Or that he felt guilty about us already having slept together.

"I have a proposition for you." One corner of his mouth twitched. "A business proposal."

"Okay. Will the office work?"

Alix nodded and led the way. He sat down in the chair in front of the desk and set one of the coffees on the desk. I put one of the drinks I bought in front of him and then walked around behind the desk. It felt strange, us sitting like this, as if he was the employee and I the employer, but I wasn't going to do anything to change it. I needed the desk between us for both distance and perspective.

"I have a contract for you," he said, gesturing to the papers on my desk. "Two, actually. The first is to move your assistant position from temporary to full-time. Jean is taking care of things on the temp agency side, so you don't have to worry about that."

That one was on top, I saw. He fell silent as I read

through. It was fairly straightforward for a contract. A set salary – which was higher than I expected – as well as working hours, which holidays I'd have off, my new insurance provider, and a week's worth of paid leave gained every two years up to six weeks off total. When I got to the part about how the first week would be available as soon as I signed, I stopped and looked up.

"This is too much."

I waited for him to admit that he'd given me such a generous contract because he and I had slept together, but he just shrugged.

"I don't really know what it says. I had Jean write it up so I wouldn't be tempted to try to bribe you."

My eyes narrowed. "Bribe me for what?"

He smiled. "Bribe you to sign the second contract. It's the same as every other model contract I have, so you don't have to worry about favoritism there."

I set aside the assistant contract and started going through the other one. I managed to keep my expression neutral even as my brain struggled to accept the numbers I was reading. He set it up for me to be paid per session, as he'd said, with the first two 'test' sessions I'd already done being only a little less than any future sessions would be. With each session, I'd have a release form to sign, which gave me a bonus. A bonus that made each session worth more than I made at the temp agency in a month. If I declined to sign the release forms, any photos from that session would only be available to Alix to use privately, unless I wished to purchase them.

The way my stomach tightened told me that the idea of him hanging my photos on the walls of his apartment, or wherever he lived, was almost as nerve-wracking as having them on display.

The contract also allowed for the option to release only photos that didn't show my face. I'd receive a smaller bonus than if I agreed to allow them all to be used, but it also kept me from having an all-or-nothing decision to make.

"This is the same contract all your models sign?"

Alix stiffened, making me wonder if it was me questioning, or if it was the fact that I said *all your models*.

"I'm not treating you any differently," he said, the muscles in his jaw clenching. "I want you to model for me *and* be my assistant. If you would prefer one over the other, that's your choice."

I was struck by the strange impulse to reach across the desk and touch him, reassure him. I curled my hand into a fist.

"It just seems like a lot," I said carefully. "I didn't come to the States to be a model, or to make a lot of money."

He raised an eyebrow. "You're hesitating because I'm offering too much?"

When he said it like that, I felt pretty foolish, but I had to know. "Why me?"

Alix stood, his hand rubbing the back of his neck. "I thought we talked about this."

I shook my head. "I know you think I don't see myself clearly, but it's not about that. We've done a couple sessions, but this contract says that you want me to do a whole new line. You mentioned it before, and I asked a similar question. You didn't really answer me then, and I would like an answer now. Why do you want me to pose for a whole new line instead of hiring a professional?"

I was feeling pretty good about how matter-of-fact I sounded, but the piercing look Alix shot me made me think twice, and his gaze didn't waver as he walked around to stand in front of me.

"I want you to be the model for my new series because you're the inspiration behind it. The only one I can see in my head when I picture it."

I stared at him. I didn't know what the new series was, but how could *I* have been an inspiration for anything?

"Alix, I–"

He crouched in front of me, putting us at eye level. He reached out, tucked a curl behind my ear.

"Hear me out about it, at least?"

Dammit.

I nodded. How could I say no to a job that could give me enough money that I'd never again have to worry about failing here and having to return to Ireland? A job that would allow me to have a savings account for emergencies, something to fall back on if I needed it.

He pulled his chair around the desk so that we were sitting on the same side of it, our knees almost touching.

"You already know that I enjoy bondage."

That sentence shouldn't have made me need to press my thighs together.

"Well, I like doing more than that." He kept his eyes on my face as he spoke, and I got the impression that he was waiting for me to freak out. "I'm into the whole BDSM package, and I want to do an entire series on it."

I held up a hand. "You want me to pose for even kinkier pictures than me in my underwear with my hands tied?"

Alix chuckled. "When you say it like that..."

I crossed my arms and leaned back, waiting for him to realize I was only half-joking.

He ran his hand over the dark stubble on his chin. "Sorry. I'm just not used to having to explain it. Usually, the...*people* I'm talking to already know about the lifestyle."

I was grateful he didn't go into detail about just who those *people* were. Even though I wouldn't be sleeping with him again, that didn't mean I wanted to hear about the women he'd been with before me. Or the women he'd be with in the future. The ones who *already knew* what that lifestyle was already about.

"You want to do a series of photographs showing the BDSM lifestyle. With *me*." I had to say it out loud to see if it freaked me out or not. Judging by the rush of arousal that coursed through my veins, I would have to say...not.

"More or less," Alix said. "The conditions the contract spelled out stay the same. No nudity. And what you said before, about things staying professional between us, that's still there too."

I knew if I took the time to think through it, I'd find a dozen reasons why I should tell Alix that I'd be his assistant and nothing more. I didn't ask for time, but I did have a question.

"Before I can yes or no, I need one thing."

"What's that?"

I pressed my hands against my stomach, wishing they could calm the butterflies. "I need to know exactly what you'll be expecting from me."

He was quiet for a minute, then stood. "Take the rest of the day off. Tonight, I'll take you somewhere for *research*."

I may not have been overly experienced sexually, but even I could guess that wherever he was taking me, my work clothes wouldn't cut it.

This was going to be...interesting.

13

ALIX

Deciding to take Sine to Gilded Cage felt right in a way that made me more than a little nervous. My friends and I didn't bring girls to the club, but after Erik had broken the ice and brought Tanya, we'd assured him we didn't mind.

Which meant it wouldn't be an issue for any of the rest of us to do the same. Not that this was the same. This was just business, I'd promised myself.

That promise lasted until I knocked on the door and Sine opened it.

Shit.

Fuck.

I hadn't told her how to dress because I honestly hadn't thought of it, but if I had, I never would have imagined *this*.

She wore no make-up, but the fresh-faced look worked for her. Her curls were as wild as they ever were, and I liked that she hadn't tried to tame them. Comfortable-looking flats kept her at five feet, which made me remember how delicate she'd felt underneath me. Then I processed the rest of the outfit.

She was wearing shorts, but not some dressy khaki kind of things, or the baggy gym shorts she'd worn the last time I was here. They were short, ending just below her ass, but so tight that she could bend over without flashing anyone. Her shirt was made of the same clingy material, molding to her slim frame and those firm, high breasts. The neckline wasn't low, and where we were going, she'd be one of the more conservatively dressed patrons, but she would, without a doubt, draw attention. Men like me – or women like me, for that matter – would be enchanted by her.

Shit.

I didn't want anyone else looking at her. She was mine to look at.

No, not mine, I reminded myself. We'd made that clear. We weren't together. This was research so she'd feel comfortable doing the series.

Employer-employee. Photographer and model.

No matter what happened at the club, I would keep it professional. Even if that meant I had to threaten to beat the shit out of a few people. *Professionally*, of course.

"Is there something wrong with the way I'm dressed?"

I jerked my head up. "Why would you say that?"

"Because you're staring at me." She crossed her arms, drawing attention to her breasts, and making me suddenly need to adjust myself.

"Trust me," I said with a wry smile, "where we're going, I won't be the only one staring."

W<small>E WENT</small> in the middle of the week, partly because I figured the chances of the guys being here was smaller than it'd be on a weekend. I didn't want to try to explain to them who Sine was. I'd seen what happened when Tanya had come to the club when she had been Erik's editor. Erik had claimed her, right then and there, and nothing he said after that mattered. She was his, even if he hadn't been willing to admit it yet.

I wasn't sure what I would do if faced with the same situation, and I didn't think I wanted to find out. Sine and I had an understanding, and I didn't want to jeopardize that.

Still, as we made our way through the club to one of the tables at the back, I found my hand hovering over the small of her back, my instinct to protect more than guide. And hidden under that, my need to let everyone here know that she was with me.

Okay, maybe not so hidden.

"We're going to sit back there," I said, leaning down so I could speak in her ear without having to shout. "Let you get a good look at things."

She was already looking, I knew. From the moment we walked inside, she hadn't stopped looking. She didn't seem freaked out by any of it, not even when Eloise and her partner, Big Cindy, walked by in their matching leather corsets and nipple rings. Most first-timers were easy to spot. They either came in all wide-eyed and blushing, or were all swagger and arrogance.

Sine was neither.

It wasn't until I settled into the booth next to her that I realized what it was. She was paying attention. To everything. As a photographer, I knew what it was to observe, to see the world without getting involved, but I hadn't seen it from someone else. She was mentally taking notes, filing away whatever she found interesting.

"Is there anything specific you want me to focus on?" She leaned closer to speak, but didn't look at me. "Something you have in mind for your photo line?"

Right, the photo series. The reason we're here.

"I have a few things in mind," I admitted, shifting into work mode. "Nothing with the clothing." I glanced sideways at her. "I prefer what you wear."

A faint flush spread across her cheeks. "You said you didn't want to only explore bondage, right?"

I nodded. "I'm thinking of this as a sort of juxtaposition between the stereotypes of BDSM and how things really work."

She turned to me at last, curiosity rather than desire in her eyes. "Show me."

I stood and held out a hand. She took it, and I kept my fingers curled around hers. We moved around the edge of the dance floor, and I swiped my VIP card across the card reader next to the door.

When we stepped into the room and closed the door

behind us, the music faded, and I was made painfully aware that we were alone. In a room with a bed. Again.

To distract myself from how tight my jeans had become, I walked across the room to the wall where a series of whips, floggers, and crops hung.

"Every Dom who uses these has to know exactly how to use them and what sort of damage they each inflict, as well as what their Subs need." I ran my fingers over a couple of the items. "Subs aren't the only ones who need to be trained. Doms need it too. A man or woman who picks up one of these things without thoroughly understanding the responsibility they have can hurt someone."

"So, where society sees abuse and a loss of control..."

I turned as she walked toward me. "The reality is about power, pleasure, and being in control. About knowing what someone else needs, and the two of you coming together to find a connection that provides you both with what you require."

Even as I said it, I could see the way the light in her eyes flared, the hunger when I talked about power and pleasure and control. I felt it in her body when we were together but hadn't completely recognized it as the counterbalance to what I needed for myself. Not until now.

I watched her as she approached the wall, as her hands traced along each item, her eyes studying every line. With the same dedication she'd shown as my assistant, the same scrutiny she'd had in the main room of the club, she looked at and cataloged everything. She would approach being a Sub the same way.

Dammit.

I didn't want to follow her rules. I wanted my photos, but I wanted her too.

I needed to be smart about it though, or I'd lose everything.

14

SINE

I told myself to be clinical, to separate what I felt when I was close to Alix from the sexual energy in the club. We'd agreed to be professional.

That hadn't stopped me from taking the time after work to scour my favorite thrift stores to find the outfit I'd worn last night. It had been a nice compromise of sexy while still being me. The shorts had been a bit shorter than I normally liked, and the top more form-fitting, but the expression on Alix's face had been worth it.

If he'd been paying more attention to my own face, he would've seen a similar appreciation for his attire. Jeans that hugged his thighs and ass without being obscene, and a short-sleeved shirt that left no doubt to whether or not he had a six-pack.

He did.

He'd been careful at the club not to touch me, but I'd felt the heat of him as if we'd been skin to skin. A part of me had wanted to lean into him, not only so I could enjoy his touch, but also to stake a claim. He was there with *me*. It didn't matter if I'd put down rules to prevent us from crossing that line again. He'd come with me, and he'd leave with me, even if it wasn't for the reasons I wished.

I could admit to myself that I wanted him. A purely physical reaction.

At least, that's what I managed to keep telling myself until we walked out of the club and Alix had gone and done something sweet. There'd been a pair of young women in their mid-twenties giggling and swaying as the doorman flagged down a taxi, and Alix had asked me to wait for him as he went over to the cab. He'd leaned down, giving us all an eyeful of that firm ass and a strip of tanned skin at his waist, and spoken with the driver for a few minutes before straightening and coming back to me.

When I asked what he'd been doing, he almost seemed embarrassed but had still told me that he'd given the cabbie some incentive to make sure the two women arrived at their apartment safely. Naturally, I asked how he'd know if the guy followed through on his promise, and the look he'd given me said it all. Alix was a man who was accustomed to people doing what he asked – or what he ordered.

As I walked into the studio, my stomach twisted into knots, only easing when Alix appeared, his expression showing a strange sort of relief, as if he'd been afraid I wouldn't show.

"I have your contracts for you," he said, gesturing

toward the table. "You can sign both or just one." He gave me a lopsided smile that spoke volumes about how uncertain he was. "I'm just hoping you're not here to tell me to shove both jobs."

"I'm not," I promised, meeting his eyes. "I'm planning to sign both."

The statement surprised me more than it probably should have. Until that very moment, I'd still been debating the merits of modeling for him.

After I signed and initialed all the places marked out in both contracts, he spoke again, "May I ask what it was that made your decision for you?"

"Last night, when you paid the cabbie to make sure those girls arrived home safely," I answered honestly, "it reminded me of something my brothers would have done."

He gave me an odd look. "So, you agreed to be my model because I remind you of your brothers?"

I laughed, shaking my head. "Not exactly." I leaned against the counter. "One of the reasons my family didn't want me to come to the States was because they were afraid I wouldn't have anyone to look out for me. I'm the baby in the family, and with one older sister and six older brothers, that's an awful lot of looking out for."

"If I had a sister, I can't say I wouldn't feel the same way." His eyes didn't meet mine though, and I wondered exactly what was going on in his head.

"I came here for school," I continued, "so I was barely eighteen. Mam has cousins in the city, so that was the only reason she and Da didn't raise more of a fuss, but after visiting them a few weekends, I decided it was better worth my time to work rather than going out to see them. They'd all been born here and had a much more American way about them."

"I'm guessing that's a bad thing." He sounded amused.

I rolled my eyes. "I only mean that my parents had wanted me near family so I didn't lose sight of where I come from, and my cousins didn't exactly meet that standard."

"I'm not following how this connects with what happened at the club."

"I'm getting there. Don't be getting your knickers in a twist."

The teasing note in my voice had his eyebrows shooting up. Or maybe that had been my unintentional reference to his underwear. Either way, I liked that I'd surprised him.

I kept going with my story. "About two weeks after the last time I'd seen my cousins, I was working as a receptionist on the night shift at an office building downtown. One of them, Nigel, is a couple years older than me. He came by one night at the end of my shift, asked if I would get a cup of coffee with him. It was late, but Nigel and I had always gotten along, so I went. Turned out, he just wanted to borrow money. I didn't have any, which I told him when we were standing outside at three in the morning. As soon as I said it, he hailed a cab. I walked to the subway."

Alix's hand curled into fists. "He left you alone at three in the morning while he took a taxi home?"

I shrugged. "He didn't think of it as putting me in danger, I'm sure. He doesn't have any sisters."

Alix took a step toward me, eyes blazing. "I don't give a damn if he has sisters or not. I'm an only child, and I would never leave a woman alone at night, especially one..." His voice trailed off.

I looked up at him, pulse taking off at a gallop. "Especially one *what*?"

His gaze locked with mine, and I could fairly feel the electricity between us. I wanted him to finish the sentence, but at the same time, I didn't. If he said it was because I was like a little sister, or because he thought I was in more danger due to being a girl...

I wanted him to be angry because it was *me*. Because *I* was special to him.

He reached out, brushed the back of his hand down my cheek. "I'd never leave you alone like that." He took a step back. "No decent man would leave someone stranded like that."

I ran my hand through my curls and tried to get my thoughts back on solid ground. "Seeing you take the time and money to get two strangers home safely just confirmed what I already knew."

"And what was that?" His voice was soft, but I couldn't exactly call it gentle.

I didn't trust myself to do anything more than glance at

him as I answered, "That I could trust you to keep
me safe."

MY HANDS WERE above my head, wrapped from elbows to
wrists and attached to the chains hanging from the ceiling.
The ribbons were purple, the exact same shade as the bra
and panty set Alix had given me to change into. I hadn't
asked how he'd known my measurements. He was a
photographer. And he'd had his hands on my body. I
couldn't forget that.

Not even if I tried.

He was kneeling behind me now, his hands on my
ankles as he positioned my feet. At first, I'd been surprised
that he hadn't put me in heels, but then his fingers had
trailed over my calf as he explained why he wanted me in
my bare feet.

I couldn't remember what he said, but it'd been something artistic.

"A little farther." He nudged them apart. "Arch your
back a bit more. One more set and we'll call it a day."

I nodded, trying not to shift my weight as he stood and
moved back. I closed my eyes and ran through everything I
needed to do tomorrow morning in an attempt to distract
myself from the fact that he was looking at my ass.

"Keep still."

I felt him set something on the small of my back. It
didn't weigh much, but it wasn't until the soft leather strips

brushed against the tops of my thighs that I realized he'd carefully balanced a flogger on my back.

I let myself fall back into the quiet place where I waited for him to take the pictures he needed. It was a place where the discomfort in my body faded to the back of my mind, hidden under the heat of Alix's gaze, under the sounds of him breathing, walking, under the clicks of his camera.

"Did you play sports back home?"

The personal question startled me, somehow more intimate than his prior touches. If it was all about the modeling, then it was easy to tell myself that he saw me only as a prop, an object in his photographs. Not in a bad way, but in a different way.

I heard his footsteps coming toward me, then the weight of the flogger vanished. His palm was hot as it slid over my ass and up my spine.

"You're strong," he continued. "I've photographed men and women both, all different body types and sizes. I haven't only studied photography. I've taken several anatomy and biology courses, learning muscles and bones. Learning all about the body."

"I was involved in gymnastics," I said as he walked around in front of me, trying to ignore the way his hands felt on me. "And karate. I was always small, but I got into fights anyway. Da convinced Mam that if I was going to fight, I might as well know how to do it right."

He reached up and touched something that released the chain. My arms fell, but he caught them, his fingers starting to work on the simple knots he'd used to bind me.

"I played football too." I smiled as I straightened. "Soccer, I mean."

His hands moved over my arms as the ribbons fell to the ground. The pins and needles feeling that rushed through my veins as my circulation returned to normal was hazy under the electricity of his touch.

"Did your brothers play too?"

"Most of them," I said. "Callum preferred cricket."

He'd reached my fingers but wasn't letting them go. I raised my head until I was looking directly at him. Without taking his eyes from mine, he lifted my hand and kissed my fingertips.

"That–" I swallowed hard. "We talked about – we're not supposed to – Alix..."

"You said that I reminded you of your brothers." He slid a hand around my waist and pulled me to him until there was no room left between us. "I don't want to remind you of them." He lowered his head until his mouth hovered above mine. "Because what I want to do to you is most definitely *not* brotherly."

"Fuck me," I whispered as arousal shot through me.

"That's the idea."

15

ALIX

I'd tried. I really had.

But from the moment I'd stretched her bound arms above her head, I'd known I was in trouble. Bondage was more my thing than punishment, but seeing that flogger resting just above the swell of her ass tempted me in a way nothing else had.

By the time I finished taking the last few shots, my cock had been hard and aching.

I'd thought talking to her about something simple and non-sexual would help, but all it had done was make me want her more.

So I'd taken the chance.

A shudder went through me as I claimed her mouth. The taste of her, the feel. She was so small, so fragile-looking, but I'd seen the strength in her muscles, felt it in her touch. I knew she could take everything I wanted to give her. And that she could give it back just as good.

I slid my hands down her back to grip her ass and picked her up. She wrapped her legs around my waist, her thighs gripping me tight enough that I was able to raise a hand and bury it in her hair. I tugged on her curls, probably harder than I should have, but she moaned, grinding down on my painfully hard cock, and that just turned me on even more.

"Bad...idea..." Her mouth slid down my throat, teeth biting at the skin.

"Don't care." I slammed her back against the wall, letting my arm take the majority of the hit.

"Me either." She put her mouth against my ear, her accent thick as it flowed over me. "Are you wanting to tie me up again? Or was there more you wanted to be doing to me?"

I closed my eyes for a moment. Was she fucking *kidding* me?

"Are you sure?" I couldn't look at her as I asked the question.

I felt her smile against my neck, then she raised her head, those gorgeous eyes of hers sparkling.

"How else will you be making me behave myself?" She shifted her weight, rubbing against me.

"Fuck," I growled as I grabbed her hips. "Stop."

"Make me."

I'd already learned that setting a challenge for her made her rise to the occasion, and Sine's words touched on that primal part of me that thrived on control, prompting me to want to do exactly what she said.

Make her stop.

I spun us around, finding the couch with ease. I sat us both down, manhandling her until she was draped over my lap, ass in the air. The panties I'd chosen for her were the sort that left enough of those firm muscles bare to be distracting.

I ran my hand over the pale flesh, enjoying the freedom to touch her without an artistic excuse. She wriggled on my lap and looked over her shoulder at me. One eyebrow went up, and something inside me snapped at the challenge.

I brought my hand down, palm smacking against skin hard enough to sting. She gasped, eyes widening, and I waited. It was one thing to do a little light bondage. Spanking wasn't exactly hardcore, but it wasn't for everyone. I rarely did it, and it was the furthest I usually ventured into pain.

"Is that all you've got?" She grinned at me.

Two quick slaps to her ass made her whimper, but she didn't pull away. Her hands curled against the couch, and I reached for the clasp of her bra. A flick of my fingers and I was pulling it off.

"Hands behind your back."

She did as I asked without a moment's pause, and I used the bra to bind her wrists. I ran my hand up between her shoulder blades, then buried my fingers in her hair again. The sound that escaped made me chuckle, and that turned into a full laugh when she glared at me.

"You sound like a fucking cat." I moved my fingers,

massaging her head, and bringing another one of those sounds. "Like you're purring."

She laughed, a rich, throaty sound that made me want to take her hard and fast until she screamed my name.

But first, I intended to leave her ass a beautiful shade of red before I finally buried myself inside that tight, wet heat of hers.

"If it gets to be too much, say–"

"Rugby."

I paused with my hand in the air. "What was that?"

"Rugby," she repeated. "Safe word, right? Not something I'd normally be yelling out in the heat of the moment."

I chuckled, my heart squeezing for a moment. Sex had never been like this for me before. Something that had humor as well as arousal. Perhaps that was what I'd been missing, what made Sine inspire me. She possessed both the innocence and sexuality that had prompted my line, so it made sense that she had other seemingly contradictory characteristics.

"Let's see exactly what I *can* get you to yell."

The answer was a litany of curse words that I reasoned could be blamed on her brothers.

My hand was burning, but I doubted it was anywhere close to the heat she was feeling. And yet, when I slid my hand between her legs, her panties were soaked. I pressed my fingers against the wet cloth, increasing the pressure and friction until she cried out, body stiffening.

I took advantage of her post-orgasm haze to move her. I

needed to be inside her, but I knew I couldn't count on being with her again, so there was something I needed to do, something I'd been fantasizing about from the first time I'd tied her up.

The pillows and cushions I used as props offered her a soft place to lay while I changed her restraints. No longer were her hands tied behind her back. Instead, I bent her legs out to the side, a position that would've been difficult for someone without Sine's background in gymnastics. I then tied her wrists to her ankles until she was spread open and exposed, her pussy glistening, pale pink nipples already hardened into little points.

It was too bad she wouldn't pose nude for me because this image was pure beauty. Even as I thought it, a bolt of jealousy went through me. No. I didn't want her posing like this for the camera. No one else should have the privilege to see this part of her. And it wasn't just her body. It was the open look of trust she gave me as I bound her.

That was *mine*.

I couldn't take my eyes off her as I stripped, and the way her gaze followed my every move assured me that I wasn't the only one greedy to drink my fill. I shrugged out of my shirt, then yanked off my jeans.

My erection sprang free, throbbing and aching, but I resisted the urge to touch myself. I went to my knees, resting my hands on my thighs as I traced every line of her body with my gaze. I'd always appreciated the artistic view of the submissives I'd been with in the past, but Sine transcended them. There was no fear on her face, only desire and trust. A good sub would have those things too, but with her, it went beyond the physical.

"I'm going to go down on you," I said matter-of-factly. "But don't come until I give you permission."

"How in the bloody hell am I supposed to stop from coming?"

The expression on her face made me chuckle. "Should we make it a bet?"

She glared at me. "What do I get when I win?"

Her question made me realize that I had a way to ensure that this wouldn't be our last time together.

"*If* you win," I said, "at a time and place of your choosing, I'll give you no fewer than three orgasms."

Her eyebrows went up. "That sounds to me like a reward for you as well."

I lifted a hand and wiggled my fingers. "I'll do it with just my fingers and mouth."

"You're quite certain of yourself, aren't you now?"

"I am." I maneuvered myself so that I was crouched down low enough to reach her with little effort.

"And what will be happening *if* I lose?" she countered.

I met her gaze as I slid my hands under her ass and raised her hips ever so slightly. "At a time and place of *my* choosing, I get to fuck your ass."

Her mouth fell open, and I watched her expression for signs of disgust. When I didn't see any, I flicked out my tongue and lightly traced the sensitive skin at the top of her mound.

"Do we have an agreement?" I asked.

She nodded, then let out a startled cry as I dove in. One day, I planned to take my time with her, slowly drawing out her pleasure until she was sobbing and begging for relief. Right now, however, I was determined to win, and my plan of action was to assault her body with so much stimuli that she'd be unable to compose herself enough to fight off her body's natural response.

I held her in place as she tried to squirm, whether to get me closer or push me away, I didn't know. Unless she used the safe word, I was doing what I wanted, and I trusted her to know when it got to be too much.

I used the flat of my tongue to lick her before moving my main focus to her clit. A lot of men, unfortunately, tended to focus on a woman's vagina. Sure, a woman could experience pleasure from attention there, especially if a man knew how to find her g-spot, but the clitoris was the best place to work some magic, especially when it came to oral sex.

Her body rocked as I teased her clit, alternating tongue and teeth with just enough differing pressure to keep her from getting used to it. I felt her muscles tensing as she tried to move her legs and arms, fingers curling as they sought for something to dig into. When I was certain she realized that she had no way of controlling what I did – short of stopping things completely – I put my mouth over her clit and applied the hard suction that had always gotten me results in the past.

She was no exception.

"Fuck!" She practically screamed the word, her hips jerking. "Alix. *Please!*"

I hummed laughter and let the vibrations add to her torment.

"Oh fuck." Her back arched, muscles spasming as she tried to fight back what I knew was inevitable. "Please, Alix."

"Please what?" I asked, drinking in the sight of her flushed skin, her desperate expression.

"Please let me come."

I pressed my mouth against her inner thigh, sucking until I left a mark. "Why would I do that?" I asked.

"Alix." The word came out as a whine, but it was the kind of sound that made my neglected cock perk up and take notice.

"We made a bet that you could hold off coming until I gave you permission," I reminded her. "But we never said that I had to give it as soon as you asked."

"Bastard," she growled at me.

"Let's get back to it, shall we?"

After nearly two full minutes of garbled curses in an accent so thick I could barely understand any of her words, she came with a scream.

As much as I wanted to gloat, I needed to be inside her more. I straightened into a more comfortable position and adjusted my grip as I lifted her. I hesitated for a moment to give her the chance to say the word, but when she didn't do anything more than moan my name, I slammed into her.

She cried out again, eyes flying open so that her gaze

met mine. I held it as I wrapped my fingers around her shoulders. She was so small that it was easy for me to move her to meet my thrusts, each one hard enough to drive a burst of air from her lungs.

She came a second time, the ripples of her muscles around my cock sending me racing to the edge. I fought my body, determined to give her at least one more climax, but as she chanted my name, I satisfied myself with knowing that I was drawing out the one she was having now, and then I let go.

I clutched her to me as white-hot pleasure raced through my veins. I couldn't say what I wanted from her, or even really what I felt, but the one solid thing I knew to be true was that the woman in my arms had knocked my world off its axis, and nothing would ever be the same.

16

SINE

I stretched but didn't throw off my covers. I had the air conditioning on a low enough temperature that I was usually able to sleep comfortably with a sheet and a light blanket, but I'd woken up yesterday wrecked and aching. By noon, I was coughing, and my head ached. With my new job and responsibilities, I couldn't afford to be ill, so I forced myself to the closest free clinic. I'd gotten back hours later, even more miserable than before, but at least fortified with medication and vitamins.

I'd hoped I would wake up mended today, but that was wishful thinking on my part. I wasn't ill often, but when I was, it hit me hard. Da had always said it was because I pushed myself until something had to give.

I rubbed my forehead and glanced over at my clock. It was almost time to take my medicine again. I didn't want to get up, but I'd purposefully left it in the bathroom so I'd have to do just that.

I splashed some water on my face before retrieving what I needed. As I shut the cabinet door, I caught sight of my reflection and grimaced. Good thing it was still the weekend. I didn't quite understand why Alix thought I was a good model, though the pictures I'd seen showed a woman different than the one I saw in the mirror. But now, even he would be unable to find anything attractive in how I looked.

A warmth spread through me at the thought of Alix, and I allowed myself a smile. I didn't know exactly what we were doing, but I'd thoroughly enjoyed our post-session sex Thursday afternoon, and if I was being honest, I wouldn't mind more of it. I always thought I wasn't the sort of person who would really enjoy sex since I hadn't particularly liked it with the two guys I'd slept with before Alix, but he was making me reconsider that way of thinking.

Even the memory of my time with Alix wasn't enough to keep me on my feet for long though. I wrapped my blanket more tightly around my shoulders and shuffled into the kitchen. I heated up one of those pre-packaged bowls of soup that never tasted as good as what Mam made, retrieved a bottle of water, and then made my way into the living room.

I managed to eat and drink most of my meal, but not too long after I finished, I fell back asleep. It was my phone ringing that woke me from a dreamless sleep. It'd already gone to voicemail by the time I managed to get awake enough to grab it from the table, but Mam's number still showed on the screen, so I tapped the callback option before she could wait her usual five minutes and call again.

That had always been Mam's way. If we didn't answer when she called, she wouldn't give up until she got ahold of us. One time, when my brother Ian had been out with some friends, he hadn't answered her call, so she'd driven to the pub. There he was, chatting up some girl when Mam came in wearing a housecoat, her hair in curlers. Our tiny mother had grabbed his ear and dragged him out, then took him straight to the local priest and waited outside while Ian was in confession.

"Morning, Mam," I said as soon as she answered.

"What's wrong with ya, darlin'?"

Her familiar voice washed over me, and I closed my eyes as a wave of homesickness followed. It was times like these that I missed my mother.

"Not feelin' well, Mam." Whenever I talked to either of my parents, especially her, I sounded like I'd never left home.

"Are ya eatin' enough?"

"Yes, Mam." I smiled as she began her usual line of questioning. I knew it all by heart, but I let her go about it anyway. It was nice to have someone make a fuss for once.

I settled back onto the couch and snuggled down into my little nest of blankets. It wasn't as good as Mam being here to take care of me, but listening to her fuss was a nice consolation prize.

"Are ya sure yer takin' care of yourself, Sine?"

"I am, Mam," I promised for the third time.

"Now tell me more about this job Donald mentioned."

I mentally cursed my favorite brother while I tried to figure out the best way to explain things to my mom without her freaking out. "I'm working as an assistant to a photographer."

"That's lovely, dear. What's her name?"

Another curse to Donald.

"His name's Alix Wexler. And before you ask, he's a nice young man, Mam."

"Is he of the faith?"

I stifled a laugh. "I don't believe so. We don't really talk about that sort of thing."

And there was no way in hell I'd be telling my mam what it was the two of us *did* talk about, because that was not the sort of thing that was fit conversation between mother and daughter. Especially when said mother would probably fly here and drag me to church if she ever found out what I was doing.

"Does he treat you well?"

I was pretty certain that her idea of *treating me well* didn't include the multiple orgasms he'd given me, but I'd just leave it at an affirmative answer.

"Yes, Mam, he does."

"If he ever..."

"Mam." I sighed.

She kept going, just like I'd known she would. "You listen to me, Sine Janet McNiven, there may be an ocean between us, but your family will always be there when you need us. Are ya hearin' that?"

"Yes, Mam." I sniffled, suddenly realizing that I'd teared up.

As we finished up our conversation, I promised myself that part of that insane amount of money that Alix was paying me would go toward a ticket for a trip back home. But just a trip. I was more determined than ever to remain in America for life.

17

SINE

I 'd called off work yesterday, even though I hated doing it. I never liked missing work, even when I hadn't enjoyed what I was doing. What was happening between Alix and me made it harder. Especially when he hadn't answered his phone either time I'd called. Not wanting to seem desperate, I simply left him a voicemail saying that I was sick and hoped that his not answering hadn't been due to any awkwardness about what happened last week. We'd been fine together on Friday, but there was always the chance that he'd been acting and the weekend had given him the time to reconsider.

My palms were sweating as I approached the studio. I wasn't assuming or asking for anything, but I had two contracts with Alix, so I could walk in there without anything but work on my mind, and it wouldn't be a lie.

Not entirely.

The door was locked when I reached it, but that wasn't out of the norm. If Alix was focused on something, he didn't always remember to check the time. I punched in the code he'd given me for instances such as this, then went inside.

I made it halfway across the main floor before I realized I wasn't alone.

"Sine, right?"

A woman's voice came from the couch. I mustered a polite smile as I turned to see Giselle lounging there. She had that fake casual thing going on, the kind that said it took a lot of work to be so nonchalant.

"Good morning, Giselle," I said.

She fluttered her red tipped fingers at me. "When Alix heard my job was completed, he asked me to come back in and finish up his series."

Was she talking about *my* series? The one he'd said I'd inspired? The one that he hadn't been able to see anyone else doing?

"I'll leave you two to it, then." I nodded at her before turning and heading to my office.

Alix didn't owe me anything. The contract for modeling had been at his discretion. Either one of us had the ability to end it whenever we wished. It was for that reason we had a second contract for my work as his assistant, so that even if he chose to discontinue the series, or it reached its natural conclusion, I would still have a job.

Giselle was a professional. It made sense that Alix would want to work with her. My own time in front of the camera had been a fluke, nothing more. I'd told myself that every time I was there, and I thought I'd been listening.

I never imagined how much it would sting to see Alix move to another model. Then again, it was coming as quite a surprise. If it had happened right after we slept together the first time, I would've thought that he'd gotten what he wanted. But we'd proven that sex hadn't needed to change anything.

Or that's what I'd thought, anyway.

But that wasn't what I needed to focus on. I'd been gone yesterday, and I needed to get caught up on things. If I fell too far behind, I could lose this job too. And this was a job I was qualified to perform, one I liked and felt competent doing.

So, I did what I did best. I organized and filed and attended to all the little details that most people let fall through the cracks.

I flipped on the radio and tried not to think about what Alix and Giselle were doing on the other side of my door. A door I'd closed on the off chance that they were saying things I didn't want to hear.

Like how foolish Alix had been to think that I could give him the sort of quality work that could compare to anything Giselle could provide.

I didn't think Alix would be cruel, but an admission

such as that, no matter how kindly spoken, would still hurt. Better to keep my dignity through ignorance than be hurt by some innocuous remark from someone I'd come to consider, at the very least, a friend.

The hours crept by as I struggled to keep from glancing at the clock every five minutes. By the time eleven o'clock came, I couldn't wait any longer for lunch. I needed to get some air.

I felt a bit childish, opening the door a crack and listening, but I didn't want to risk walking out into something that would only lead to embarrassment for all involved. When I didn't hear anything, I ventured out, not taking my usual care to keep my steps as quiet as possible so as not to disturb Alix when he was working. I preferred to err on the side of giving them time to finish whatever it was they were doing, professionally or otherwise.

I didn't see Alix when I entered the main studio area, but Giselle was difficult to miss. She lay sprawled out on the pillows in the usual staging area, those ebony curls of hers spread out, and every inch of her perfect skin visible.

So much for not taking nudes.

"I hope we didn't bother you," Giselle said with a self-satisfied smile. "Things were getting a bit...noisy out here, what with all the moving things around."

"I had the radio on," I said, keeping my tone even.

"Are you going for lunch?" she asked, lazily stretching her arms above her head.

"Do you or Alix want anything?" I asked, refusing to react to her attempts at baiting me into making a scene.

"Well, we did work up an appetite," she said with a self-satisfied smirk. "But I'm not sure if he's ready to take a break yet."

"I'll ask him myself," I said, my stomach clenching at yet another innuendo. "Just to be sure."

She shrugged, then stretched lazily, her full breasts rising and falling. "He's in the bathroom cleaning up. Well, that and making sure I didn't draw blood." She wiggled her fingers at me, manicured nails painted a rich crimson. "I may have gotten a little carried away. You understand how that goes, right?"

My stomach heaved. She had to be guessing because Alix never would have told her that he and I had slept together. Unless it'd been brought up in the context of how he moved on from me so sex with her wouldn't be stepping on anyone's toes. Maybe I'd had it all wrong from the beginning. Maybe Alix had been playing me from moment one and Giselle was looking out for me.

Either way, I refused to show either of them how my insides were being torn up.

"If either of you changes your mind and want me to bring something back for you, just give me a call." I made my words even and mild, without a hint of what was lurking below the surface of my skin. Then I turned and walked away, my pace deliberately unhurried, as if I wasn't dying to rush outside so I didn't risk seeing Alix.

I'd known this was a bad idea from the beginning, so I didn't have anyone to blame but myself. The only bright side I could see was that Mam wouldn't be able to give me her usual *I told you so.*

It didn't prevent me from hearing the words echo through my head anyway, each one reminding me of how I screwed up.

"What the *hell* did you do?"

I blinked. "Have we progressed past civilized greetings now, Jean?"

Her voice didn't soften any. "When you do exactly the opposite of what I ask you to do, yes, I move past being civilized."

I was thoroughly confused, but I took a moment to watch the town car disappear around the corner before turning away from the window.

"I have no idea what you're talking about."

I picked up the wine glasses and carried them to the sink while I waited for an explanation.

"You have no idea why I got a call from your assistant slash model telling me that you'll need a new assistant, and that she doesn't plan to sign the release papers for the photos you've already taken?"

I frowned. "What?"

"That's exactly what I said."

Her words ran through my brain again, but I didn't understand them anymore this time than I had the first time.

"I'm serious, Jean. I don't know what you're talking about."

I'd intended to clear the table while I was on the phone, but now all I could think was that something had gone terribly wrong.

"Why don't you start from the beginning?" I suggested.

Jean let out a huff of air. "Sine McNiven. The assistant you didn't want. The one I told you to behave yourself with. The one you decided to turn into a half-naked model."

"I know who she is," I snapped.

"Good," Jean snapped right back, "because I was starting to wonder if you'd hit your head or been on drugs or something."

A little flare of panic went off. Jean had always been tough, and she'd never put up with any shit from me, but I'd never heard her like this before. She was genuinely pissed at me.

"What happened to Sine?" I found my fingers tightening on my phone.

"She called me about twenty minutes ago and said that she wouldn't be able to work for you anymore, that she was sorry, but you would need to find a new assistant. When I asked her why, she said that she realized it's not a good fit."

Not a good fit? What the hell did *that* mean?

"Then she said that she had second thoughts about posing for you, that her religious mother would have a heart attack if she ever found out about it."

"And you just let her hang up after that?"

Silence.

I backpedaled. "I'm sorry. That was rude of me."

"Yes, it was."

"This is all just catching me off-guard," I admitted. "I wasn't in the studio today, and she called in sick yesterday."

"Where were you today?"

"My parents came to the city to surprise me." I ran my hand through my hair. Was it possible that less than fifteen minutes ago, I'd seen them off? It seemed like a lifetime had passed. "I put a note on the studio door. I figured that Sine would appreciate another day off since she wasn't feeling well."

"So, you didn't do anything to piss her off?"

"Not that I know of." I racked my brain, trying to think of anything I could have possibly done to make Sine want to quit. "We were fine the last time I saw her."

"When was that?"

"Friday afternoon, when we left the studio." I didn't even have to think to know the answer.

After our Thursday session...encounter...whatever label I gave it, I'd worried that Friday would be awkward, but it'd felt fine to me. I'd been tempted to push my luck and kiss her again, coax her into sleeping with me again, but she'd looked exhausted, so I simply smiled and told her to rest up.

"And you said she was sick yesterday?"

"Most of the weekend, based on the voicemail she left me. She looked tired on Friday."

Jean sighed. "And you didn't talk to her directly? Not since Friday. When she started feeling sick. Seriously, Alix?"

She had that same sort of exasperated sound that my mother got when I did something stupid.

"Do you call all of your employees at home if you think they're sick?" I asked, disliking the defensive tone in my words.

There was a beat of silence before she spoke again. This time, however, her voice was soft. "She's not just any employee though, is she?"

My chest tightened. Jean was right. Sine wasn't just another model, or some random person hired to organize things for me. She wasn't my girlfriend, but she deserved to have someone look after her. And I hadn't done that.

Fuck.

I knew better.

The very core of being a good Dom was taking care of my submissive, and I hadn't done that. It didn't matter that we'd only been together a few times and that we weren't a couple. She was more than some random fuck at Gilded Cage, or some girl I hired to pose for me.

"And she didn't say why she was quitting?" I ran my

hand through my hair. "I mean, she didn't say that I did something...wrong?"

"No," Jean admitted. "But I figured you must have because I didn't believe for a minute that she hadn't thought it all through before signing."

"Shit," I muttered.

"So, you *did* do something."

Yes. I fucked her. More than once. In kinky ways. And I wanted to do more.

"No," I lied.

"Then you better get your ass over to her place, apologize, and get her back."

I scowled even as I looked for my shoes. "I said I didn't do anything."

"And I've turned forty-five for the past decade."

I couldn't remember Sine's address. "Shit."

"I'm hoping that's because you know you screwed up and not as a commentary on my age." Jean's voice was dry, but didn't sound pissed anymore, so that was good.

"I'll take care of it," I said. "I just have to find my phone. I have Sine's address in it and now I can't–"

"You're talking on it."

I closed my eyes. "Yes. Yes, I am. Sorry, my parents showing up just really threw me."

"If you want to pretend that's what it is, I won't stop you."

"Jean..."

"Let Sine know that I won't be calling around for any replacements unless she comes in to see me herself."

The call ended, leaving me staring at the phone and wondering when the hell my life had completely spun out of control.

19

SINE

When I'd gone back to the studio, Giselle and Alix had been nowhere to be seen, so I'd just gone to my office and done the work I'd been hired to do. The whole time, my brain had been going round and round with all sorts of ideas about what my next move should be. Alix hadn't done anything wrong, so I had no right to be angry at him. Things had been perfectly clear regarding our roles.

That didn't stop me from being hurt though. Hurt that I'd been replaced. That the things I thought we both felt hadn't existed. Or, rather, that they'd been one-sided.

All of that was my fault though. I was the one who'd thought Alix and I had been moving toward something real. And I hadn't even admitted that to myself until I'd seen Giselle.

By the time I'd gotten home, I'd known I couldn't subject Alix to whatever awkwardness I'd bring to work because of my own errors in judgment. He already had his new model. He didn't need my pictures, and he didn't need me.

I wouldn't have the money for a visit home now, but maybe a longer venture back was in my future. My lease would be up soon, and if I didn't find a roommate or a better paying job, I'd need to worry about where to live. And if I couldn't find a job, I'd be shipped back to Balbriggan.

But that was a problem for tomorrow.

Today, I intended to enjoy my stew and biscuits. Take a hot bath. Do some reading.

And *not* think about Alix Wexler one single bit.

My resolve lasted until the moment someone knocked on my door, and I heard his voice.

"Sine, we need to talk."

Dammit.

I couldn't bring myself to be rude when he'd done nothing wrong, so I opened the door and gestured for him to come inside. I didn't look at him though. I wasn't ready for that just yet. I needed a moment to compose myself. I hadn't planned on seeing him today.

I was just glad I hadn't done my bath yet because I would have felt a lot more vulnerable than I already did. I was still wearing the skirt and blouse I'd worn to work this morning, my only concession to comfort was my lack of shoes.

"Why'd you quit?"

No small talk. Straight to the point.

At least this would be short.

I took a deep breath and tried to keep it all as simple as possible. "I told Ms. Holloman that I was willing to work until she found someone new, so I'll have everything organized and in place for whoever comes next."

"That doesn't answer my question." He took a step toward me. "And you're not just my assistant."

"You made the right call." I tried a different approach. "Rehiring Giselle now that she's finished with her prior engagement. I'm sure she'll be perfect for the series."

"Giselle?" He frowned, the look on his face so completely baffled that I wondered if perhaps I'd gotten things wrong.

"She and I spoke earlier today," I continued. "She explained things, and I don't wish for you to feel awkward about changing your mind. I thought leaving–"

"Sine."

I shivered at the way he said my name. No one should be allowed to make two syllables sound like that.

"Start at the beginning."

Why couldn't he just let it go?

I sighed and did as he asked. "When I arrived at the studio this morning, Giselle was there. She told me that her previous job was done and that you'd asked her to come back to finish the series." I kept my voice level and flat. It was a recitation of facts, nothing more.

"Sine, I didn't–"

"It's all right," I cut him off. "And I'm sorry for not telling you directly. You were just...otherwise occupied when I left for lunch, and then neither of you were there when I came back–"

It was his turn to interrupt. "I wasn't there at all."

I stopped, mouth open as whatever I'd been planning to say died before it could get out. It took me a moment before I was able to ask, "What?"

He took another step toward me, his hand coming out to lightly touch my arm. "I was with my parents all day today. I left a message."

I shook my head. "I didn't get a text from you."

A sheepish expression crossed his face. "I misplaced my phone."

I raised an eyebrow.

"I know," he said. "It sounds like some sort of con, but I promise that it's not. Last night, I was doing some re-arranging at my place, and I misplaced my phone. I didn't realize it until my parents showed up here for a surprise visit, but I didn't find it again until a couple hours ago."

The light in his eyes was so earnest, I wanted to believe him. But I couldn't. Not yet. I still had questions.

"I swear, Sine, on the way to breakfast, I stopped at the studio and put a note on the door saying you could have the day off. Giselle must have removed the note." He scowled. "I won't be working with her again."

"How did she get inside then?" I asked.

"I give models guest codes that I usually remove once the job's done. I must have forgotten to remove hers since her contract ended early."

He had an answer for everything, and that should have

made me suspicious, but it didn't. While odd, his version of events better fit with the character of the man I'd gotten to know.

"What did you mean when you said I was 'otherwise occupied?'"

I flushed as I answered, "Giselle said you were in the bathroom, um, cleaning up."

For a moment, he looked puzzled, and then realization dawned. "You think Giselle and I..." He shook his head. "No. Never."

"She was naked. What was I supposed to think?" I shifted my weight, unable to look him in the eye. "I mean, you and I–"

I felt him move rather than saw it, my entire body sent buzzing with awareness as he closed the distance between us. He gripped my chin, turning my face back to him. Without my shoes on, I was so much shorter than him that I had to bend my head far back so I could see his face.

"I don't sleep with my models." A smile curved one side of his mouth. "At least I hadn't until you came along."

His face was more open than I'd ever seen it, and I read the truth of his statement there.

"Maybe it would've been better if you'd stuck with that policy," I said. "A lot less trouble."

He brushed a couple curls back from my face. "I don't mind a wee bit of trouble."

His attempt at an Irish accent made me laugh, easing the negative tension between us. His fingers lingered on my cheek, the gleam in his eyes shifting to a simmer. A coil of heat inside my belly warmed me all the way through.

I pushed myself up on my tiptoes, wrapping my arms around his neck so I could pull him down to me. As soon as he realized what I was doing, he met me halfway, his mouth crashing against mine with bruising force. I didn't wait for him to take the lead. Instead, I parted my lips and traced the seam of his mouth with my tongue. He growled as his mouth opened, tongue twisting with mine.

He gripped my ass and lifted me, tugging at my skirt to give me the freedom to wrap my legs around his waist. I'd spent so much of my childhood and adolescence wishing I was taller, but with Alix, like this, I was the perfect size.

I let out a squeak as he spun us around until my back was against the door. His mouth moved down my jaw and throat, biting and sucking hard enough to make me wonder if he was leaving marks. Or if I even gave a damn.

"I don't know if I can be gentle." The rough words ghosted over my skin.

I gripped his hair and pulled his head back so that his eyes met mine. "Then don't."

"Sine..."

"I can take it," I said. "I *want* to take it."

He hesitated a moment longer, giving me the chance to back out. When I didn't, he claimed my mouth again, his hands working between us so that in only a few quick movements, he was thrusting into me, filling me completely in one motion.

I cried out, but he swallowed that noise, and every

other sound I made after it. I couldn't quiet myself as he drove into me over and over, not waiting for me to adjust or assure him that I was ready. It was rough and aggressive, a blind, primal need, and it matched my own.

I needed him like this. Needed to feel him stretching me to the point of pain while knowing I had the power to stop him with a single word. Because I didn't doubt for a moment that he would stop.

He tore away the darkness that had been hanging over me since I'd seen Giselle this morning. All of her innuendos and smirks vanished as he filled me, physically and mentally and emotionally and every other way he could. It was all him and me and the world exploding in an intense pleasure that brought tears to my eyes.

I still didn't know if we had a future between us, but in this here and now, he was mine, and I could accept that.

20

ALIX

I'd come here to convince Sine to work for me again. That had been it. But just like every other time I'd had good intentions when it came to her, they went out the window as soon as she was in front of me.

I always thought my art had helped me understand addiction because it was something that could come over me and block out everything else. I could lose myself in it for hours and never notice. Photography was the only thing that had ever done that for me.

Then I met *her*.

She was my true addiction. The thing I couldn't stay away from. The only thing I'd ever needed as much as I needed my art. And it wasn't until Jean had called me that I'd allowed myself to acknowledge how important Sine was. She'd given me back an appreciation for beauty, for life, even enhanced it.

I turned around so that my back shielded her from the main spray, then tipped her chin up so I could see her face. I pushed back the wet curls that were plastered to her head, cupped her face. My thumbs brushed over her cheekbones, touched the corners of her mouth. Her lips were still swollen from my kisses, and I could already see faint impressions on her hips where I'd held her. She'd have bruises tomorrow. From me.

"What's happening in that mind of yours?" Her fingertips lightly traced my jaw.

I shook my head.

"You're frowning, Alix. What's wrong?"

I dropped my hands. "I didn't mean to be so rough."

She smiled as she reached out and took my hands, linked our fingers together. "Do I look like I didn't enjoy myself?"

I felt a little tendril of relief and hope trying to worm its way into the knot of tension inside me. "I just...it's..."

"Alix." She raised one of my hands and kissed the back of it. "I wasn't faking it, you know. I haven't had to do that with you."

I gave her a questioning look as a stab of jealousy went through me. "But you have with others?"

She released my hands and reached for a bottle of shampoo. "Do you really want to talk about past lovers?"

I scowled at her word choice. "No."

The scent of peppermint filled the shower as she squirted some of the shampoo into my hand. "Then wash my hair."

As I worked the shampoo into a lather, I massaged her scalp, closing my eyes when she moaned. After our quick fuck against the door, she'd asked me to join her in the shower, but we hadn't really talked. And we needed to. I now knew why she'd quit, but that wasn't enough.

She had to come back.

I didn't know exactly where this thing between us was going, but I knew I wasn't ready to let her go.

"I meant what I said before," I said softly. "You're the only woman I want modeling for this series."

"Alix," she began, turning toward me.

"Hear me out," I said. "I want you to model for me, and I want you to come back to work for me as my assistant."

She opened her mouth, and I put my finger over her lips. Her tongue flicked out against the pad of my finger, and I groaned.

"Let me get this out, Sine. I need to say it."

She nodded as I rinsed her hair, taking care to keep the soap out of her eyes. Only when the water ran clear did I continue.

"If you don't think you can work as my assistant because of this," I gestured between us, "I understand. And I accept if you don't want to model for me anymore. But I still want you."

Her eyes widened. "I don't understand."

"No, you don't, do you." I leaned down and kissed her forehead. "You still don't see what you're worth." I took her hands in mine. "You're my muse."

She shook her head and tried to laugh it off. "Alix–"

"Before you walked into my studio that day, I'd been struggling. I'd lost my vision, lost sight of what had made me love photography in the first place." I struggled to find the words. "But then I saw you, and I remembered."

"You're giving me too much credit," she protested.

I shrugged. "Maybe. Maybe I would have tried to do a bondage series with another model and people would have bought the photos." I gave her a partial smile. "But they wouldn't have been a part of me. Not the way these are. You wouldn't want to deprive an artist of their muse, now would you?"

The look of exasperation on her face must have been something her brothers had all seen at one time or another. But then she smiled, and I dared to hope.

"Does that mean I can tell Jean that she doesn't need to look for another assistant?" I asked, my stomach in knots as I awaited her answer.

"I suppose not." She filled her hand with shampoo. "Now, if you want me to return the favor, I'm either going to need to grow, or..."

I didn't even hesitate to lower myself onto my knees. This wasn't about a show of submission or dominance. This was an act of intimacy between two people that I'd never allowed myself to feel before. I'd always given so much of myself over to my art, that I never felt like I had any left over to give to someone else. But with her, it was different, as if whatever I gave to her came back to me.

So, I knelt in front of her and closed my eyes as she

washed my hair. When we were finished, I'd take her to bed. Feast on her until her body was ripe and ready for me. And then I would make her scream my name.

Again.

21

SINE

"**S**top fidgeting."

It was the third time Alix had reminded me to stay still, but I couldn't help myself. I respected his work and didn't want to ruin it, but something in me was feeling a bit mischievous today.

After our shower discussion two days ago, the two of us had spent several delightful hours together, making the sort of relaxed small talk I'd never imagined Alix and I could have. We laughed and chatted and had sex and ate the last of the chocolate chip cookie dough ice cream I'd bought on my way home from work. Then he'd gone home, and I'd been absurdly hopeful as I'd gone to bed. Yesterday had been all work, but it hadn't been weird. We'd actually gotten a lot done, both in the morning when I was doing the usual paperwork, and in the afternoon, we'd worked on the photograph series. I wasn't sure if it was because of what we'd done, or if I was just starting to grow into the role I played when I was in front of the cameras, but the session had gone amazingly well.

A part of me had been a bit disappointed when we'd gone our separate ways at the end of the day, with nothing more than an exchange of heated gazes. Which meant I was humming with sexual tension by the time we were ready to start photographing today.

Alix telling me what he had in store for me had only made matters worse.

Because I wasn't wearing anything. Technically, anyway. The photographs wouldn't be nudes, but what covered my body wasn't clothes either.

They were scarves. The same silk scarves he used to bind me were now artistically draped over various body parts to keep things tasteful. What they hadn't done was keep me from getting impossibly turned on when Alix needed to adjust things, which he'd done.

A lot.

"Have you changed your mind about posing nude for me?" he asked as he walked around to stand in front of me. "Because if you keep moving like that, the pictures I take will expose some...naughty bits."

I'd been on my knees for the past few minutes while he tried to decide what the best options were for the deep green bits of fabric he was using. This was the basic submissive position, he explained, and those words had twisted the part of me that responded to the world he'd shown me.

"Is that what you want of me?" I asked, shifting again

so that the scarves he had covering one of my breasts slipped. "Sir?"

His eyes narrowed, and he reached down to wrap his fingers in my hair. The grip was slightly painful, but it just made a fresh rush of arousal go through me.

"Are you teasing me?" His voice was low, dangerous.

I licked my lips. "Perhaps," I admitted.

Without a word, he turned and walked a few steps away, set his camera down on the table, then turned back to me. I swallowed hard as he pulled his shirt over his head. He was sculpted perfection, every inch of his torso carved into the sort of definition that made me want to trace each muscle with my tongue.

When his hands went to the top of his jeans, my eyes followed. A flip of a button. The slow lowering of a zipper.

"I think we need to have a little demonstration," he said as he stopped in front of me again. "A reminder of who's in charge."

I liked the sound of that.

He reached down and plucked one of the scarves off, baring my right breast. The nipple was already tight from a combination of arousal and chill, but it wasn't the cold that made me shiver as he flicked the tip hard enough to sting.

"Keep your hands at your sides," he said as he folded back his jeans, pushing them low enough to free his cock. He wrapped his hand around the shaft, stroking it with short, almost rough, strokes. "I've been half-hard all fucking day, thinking about what you'd look like with these scarves on. Taking these pictures and trying not to think about how fuckable you are, is driving me crazy."

It was nice to know that I wasn't the only one who'd been distracted.

"Open."

I parted my lips, hands clenching as he slid his cock between them. He rocked his hips as I closed my mouth around him, savoring the feel of his soft skin against my tongue. When he ran his fingers through my hair, I closed my eyes, focused everything on my non-visual senses. The weight of him, the taste. The things that made him...*mine*.

"You need to understand something, Sine." His voice was surprisingly even considering the tension I could feel in his fingers as they pressed against my scalp. "No one – *no one* – gets to see this part of you but me. When I reveal this series, I want every man and woman to covet you, want to be you or want to be with you, want to see those pieces of you that I've kept for myself."

As he tightened his grip on my hair, I opened my eyes and looked up at him to find him watching me. He eased forward, filling my mouth with as much of him as I could take. I fought the instinct to gag, dug my nails into my thighs to prevent myself from reaching for him. I trusted him not to go too far. He'd never hurt me, not intentionally.

"I mean it, Sine." He held me in place, his gaze burning into me. "This part of you is *mine*."

Just as my eyes teared up, he backed off, releasing my hair and letting me have a moment to gasp and cough. I knew he was watching me to make sure I was okay, and I was.

I was more than okay, actually. I was wet and throbbing and desperate...and trying to not read too much into what he'd said.

"Hands and knees." His voice was tight, telling me he wasn't as calm as he was trying to appear.

I did as he said, letting the scarves fall to the floor. He moved around behind me, and for a moment, I thought I would feel him slide right into me. But he didn't. I heard him moving around for a minute or so, and then he was kneeling behind me, fingers brushing against my hip.

"Last week, do you recall a certain wager between you and I regarding your ability to refrain from coming?"

I froze as the bet came rushing back to me. Particularly the part about what would happen if I lost. Because I had lost.

Which meant that I wasn't exactly surprised to feel Alix's finger dip inside my pussy, then move up to that *other* entrance.

I hissed as the tip of his finger penetrated my ass, but I didn't ask him to stop. I never thought about doing this before the moment Alix had challenged me, but if it was with him, I was willing to try anything.

"Fuck," I groaned as his finger pushed forward, its way slicked by what I assumed was lube, or something similar.

"Relax." The command was impossibly gentle and firm at the same time. "Spread your legs a bit more."

My knees slid farther apart as his finger moved in and

out, getting me used to the burning sensation that came with this sort of penetration. As I felt the second finger join the first, I tensed up, then shuddered as his other hand reached underneath me, fingers finding my clit. He moved them in slow circles, slowly building my arousal again, mingling the two sensations until I pushed back against his twisting fingers.

"Are you close?"

I nodded.

"Are you going to come with my fingers in your ass?"

I nodded once, then stopped before I did it again. "Only if you say I can."

He chuckled, and I shuddered. I loved that sound.

"Good answer."

I whimpered as he pressed his lips against the base of my spine. "May I come?"

"Only if you're ready." After a beat, he added, "When you start coming, I'm going to replace my fingers with my cock."

I was so close, I could feel my muscles quivering in anticipation, feel the pressure building until I knew I was right at the edge.

"I'm ready," I breathed. "Please, Alix."

"Come for me then."

I let the pleasure flow over my skin, through my mind. As I reached the peak, he was there, pushing inside me, steadily filling me one inch at a time, until I couldn't distinguish between the pleasure and the pain, between where I ended and he began. Tears streamed down my cheeks, and I curled my fingers against the floor, gasping for breath, my arms shaking.

He didn't stop until he was completely inside me, and then his hands were moving over my ribs, cupping my breasts, pinching my nipples, moving down between my legs, manipulating all the different parts of me until another orgasm ripped through me. Only then did he begin to move again, driving into me at a steady pace, even as he pulled me up until my back was against his chest, one arm around my waist with his fingers between my legs, the other arm across my breasts, his hand resting on my throat.

"You haunt me, Sine McNiven." His breath was hot on my cheek as he spoke. "I can't get you out of my head. I see you everywhere." He nipped at the side of my neck. "And I want you to see me. Feel me. Always."

"I do," I managed to say as I spiraled toward another climax. "I do."

When I shattered this time, he was right there with me. And he was all I saw, all I felt.

And in that moment, I knew that he had the power to break me.

W e'd gone our own separate ways after the earth-shattering orgasm and the things we'd said. The things *I* had said. She hadn't seemed upset that we hadn't talked about it, but I'd been worried enough that when Erik had called, wanting to meet me, I immediately agreed even though I rarely went out in the middle of the week.

Café Carlyle was a favorite for my friends and me when we weren't in the mood for the BDSM scene. For a lot of people, it was the perfect setting for romance, but for us, the combination of music and art suited our temperaments. Tonight, however, I barely glanced at the Marcel Vertes murals or heard the band.

Erik was already there when I arrived.

"I ordered you a Jameson," he said as I sat down across from him.

"Everything's going well with Tanya, I presume."

A smile instantly bloomed on his face, lighting up his bright blue eyes. "Better than good."

"Still in the honeymoon phase then?" I nodded to the waiter who placed my drink in front of me.

"That's just it," Erik said. "It's not like we're pretending with each other, or trying to only show our best selves. We're still learning about each other, of course, but even when there's something that annoys us, we're always coming at it from a perspective of how to adapt and compromise."

I raised an eyebrow as I took a long drink. It burned going down, settling in my empty stomach. I needed to eat something before I had much more alcohol or I wouldn't be in condition to have a decent conversation.

"I'm serious," he continued. "Before, I'd never wanted to have to work at it, but she's worth it. Worth putting in the time and the effort." He drained his glass. "I'd rather bust my ass to make things work between us than take the easy way and lose her."

I let the silence between us sit as I finished my drink. When the waiter came back, both Erik and I ordered another drink, as well as food, then waited until he walked away to continue our conversation.

"How did you know?" I blurted out the question I'd been obsessing over since the day Jean had called to tell me that Sine had quit.

"That she was worth it?" Erik asked.

I nodded. I'd been telling the truth to Sine when I said that I wasn't always so good at communicating with words. Pictures were my medium. But Erik always had a gift for saying what I couldn't and understanding things I wasn't able to say.

"The physical attraction was there right away," he said. "But even then, it wasn't the same as it was with other women. When I saw her, it was like a punch to the gut, like she was the only other person in the world."

I thought about how I'd wanted to photograph Sine from the first time I met her even though she wasn't the sort of woman who turned heads wherever she went. How when I was with her, everyone else faded away.

"And the sex...well..." He grinned at me. "I won't kiss and tell, but it wasn't the same with her either. It was like a piece of me that I'd ignored for years was suddenly there, and it made everything more real, more important...just *more*. And her subbing for me..." He shook his head as if words were actually failing him.

My stomach clenched painfully at the memory of how it felt to be in Sine's mouth, her pussy, her ass. What it was like to see her underneath me. Kneeling in front of me. On all fours. How responsive she'd been to my touch. How much she'd enjoyed the different BDSM aspects we'd explored.

"Those were the things that made me start to think that she was different, and I still didn't get it completely," he kept going. "It was when I realized I wanted to spend time with her outside of the bedroom that scared the shit out of me. I found myself thinking about her in ways that weren't just sexual. I thought about waking up next to her. Eating meals with her. Just going places and doing things. Not only date-like things but the mundane shit. Grocery shopping. Washing dishes. All that domestic stuff that I could see stretching out in front of me."

My chest constricted, and I suddenly found it hard to breathe.

Erik's eyes grew serious as they locked on to mine. "I knew she was it for me when I couldn't see a future without her. When the idea of moving forward without her killed me."

I threw back what was left of my second drink like it was a shot rather than the expensive aged whiskey that deserved to be savored. A bright edge of panic was creeping up on me, and I fought the urge to run.

"It's that Irish girl, isn't it?" he asked. "Sine. The one you brought to the club a couple weeks back."

I nodded, not trusting myself to speak. Not that it mattered. Erik could read everything.

"Have you told her?"

I shrugged as I thought of my words this afternoon. "Sort of."

"Take it from me," he said. "Make it more than *sort of*. If she really is it for you, don't be an ass like I was and try to talk yourself out of it. If she doesn't feel the same way, at least you'll know you did all you could."

If she doesn't feel the same way.

The words were like a bucket of ice water. I hadn't even thought of that. I'd been so wrapped up into what I was feeling that I never stopped to consider that she might not feel the same thing. That for her, this might just be a hot fling. Something to enjoy while it lasted.

"The worst thing you can do," Erik added, "is to hide things from her. It won't end well."

The grim tone of his words made me frown. "That sounds like you're not only talking about me and Sine."

"I'm not," he said. "Reb and Mitzi broke up."

He was giving me an out, I saw. If I didn't want to dig any deeper into what I was feeling, I could take the change in conversation, and he wouldn't say a word about it. I had too many things I needed to think about, analyze, weigh, and I wasn't ready to do that here and now.

I followed the change of subject. "Since when?"

"Beginning of June."

"No shit." I let myself relax as I started in on my meal. "Why didn't he say anything?"

Erik scowled. "He knows we never liked her, and with what went down..."

"What went down?"

He stabbed a carrot with his fork. "He caught her cheating, and it was bad enough he didn't want to tell me any more than that."

"Shit," I breathed. "I can't say it surprises me, but still."

Erik nodded. "He finally told me the other day. Said he didn't want to make a big deal about it, but I don't think he's doing well."

As our conversation turned to our friend, I pushed back the little voice in the back of my head that wondered if something like that would happen to me, if Sine wasn't the woman I thought her to be. The voice quieted, but those seeds of doubt were there, and I knew they'd take root if I gave them even the slightest bit of attention.

23

SINE

The Big Apple in late June was sunny and hot, nothing like Balbriggan was right now. I dabbed at my forehead with a tissue and wished for one of Ireland's brisk winds off the sea. It was only eight thirty in the morning, and I was already sweating as I walked from the corner to the bodega. The traffic was awful, so it made more sense to walk the short distance to get the coffee for Alix and myself, and then go on to the studio a couple blocks down.

Alix.

As it had for the last week, the thought of him made me smile.

We hadn't talked about what any of this between us was, but we'd talked about other things. Many things, actually. I had been pleasantly surprised at the conversations we'd had. He wanted to know about Ireland, having never been there. About my family and our business. Whiskey was something of which he had some knowledge, but more of the drinking kind than the making. I told him that he and my family would get along famously, but both of us had shied away from any conversation that talked about them actually meeting.

He told me about his family too. How he was an only child whose closest relative was a cousin, Erik. How his parents were older and had retired to Philadelphia, and another cousin of his, Izett, ran the family business.

The two of us came from such different worlds, and every new thing we discovered seemed to only enforce that. How we'd been raised. How we interacted with our families. Even though I was an ocean away from my family, we were still closer than he was with his. He loved them, I could see that in the way he spoke about them, but he'd always been such a solitary person. He didn't have to tell me that. I saw it in him, the way he tended to turn into himself when he worked.

Except I saw him turning more and more to me this week. A new side of him. And I'd discovered a new side of myself through him too.

Tough. Strong. Independent. Self-reliant. These were all words that I believed described me.

Submissive.

Absolutely no one who had ever met me would have called me submissive, but when I was with Alix, that word didn't frighten me. He made me feel safe, even when he was taking away my control. Or what I perceived as control, anyway. I hadn't needed him to explain that in a D/s relationship, the sub had most of the power.

I was in the middle of the line at the bodega, lost in my thoughts when my phone went off. I cursed under my breath as I scrambled through my bag. Sometimes Alix would call to ask me to pick something up on my way in.

Except it wasn't Alix.

I frowned as my brother's name flashed across the screen. It was early afternoon in Ireland, which meant Donald should have been at work, and he was always careful to not make personal calls on company time.

"Donald?"

"Sine, Mam's in the hospital."

I stepped out of line as an icy hand grabbed my heart. "What happened?" My voice was barely a whisper as I struggled for air.

"She and Da were touring the factory, and she collapsed. Patrick was there and called an ambulance. She's still unconscious."

He didn't sound panicked, but there was an edge to his voice that I didn't like. Of all my brothers, he was the one the family went to for tricky PR situations or to soothe hurt feelings. The fact that he was the one to call made me think that things were bad enough that my siblings didn't want me to freak out.

"I'm coming home."

He was in the middle of patiently explaining to me

why I didn't need to do that when I hung up on him. I didn't need to be handled. I needed to get back to my family. Immediately.

I flagged down a taxi and gave my address before pulling up a travel website on my phone. When I'd moved, I hadn't thought about what I would do if something happened to my family and I wasn't there. I'd only been thinking of myself. What *I* wanted. What would make *me* happy.

Now my mother was in the hospital, and I was thousands of miles away.

I did my best to ignore the snail's pace at which we were moving and focused on finding a flight. I needed to leave today. The flight alone would be around seven hours, and I would need at least an hour to go through all the security steps. The absolute best I could hope for was to see my parents in nine to ten hours. And that would be if everything I needed fell into place.

Even though I knew I wasn't to blame for what happened, I couldn't completely stop the guilt. I should have been there. Showing up right alongside the others. Helping care for my mother. Being there for my father. Taking care of my family. *That* was where my responsibilities were. In Ireland.

I never should have forgotten that.

I blinked back the tears as the cab pulled up in front of my building. I couldn't afford the luxury of giving in to my emotions. I had managed to put myself on standby for a flight leaving in a little over an hour, so I needed to pack. I hadn't left much behind when I moved here, and I didn't want to have to make a stop between the airport and the hospital, which meant packing was a necessity. Especially since I had no idea how long I would be there.

Or if I would return to America at all.

24

ALIX

Sine was late.

She was never late.

I kept looking at my phone, trying to figure out what the hell was going on. It was nearly eleven o'clock, and I didn't have a call or a text from her. I'd been so wrapped up in designing the next series of photos I wanted to take that I hadn't realized I was still alone until Erik had texted me about our normal Friday night thing and I'd seen the time.

I'd gone to the office to see why she hadn't stopped to say hi, but she wasn't there. For the last fifteen minutes, I'd been telling myself to keep waiting, to not make assumptions. That she must've had a good reason for not calling and telling me she was going to be late.

She was a responsible person. A hard worker. Reliable.

She wouldn't have simply blown off work.

After trying to convince myself that everything was

okay for a quarter of an hour, I decided that it was better to risk her being annoyed with me for calling to see where she was, than it would be to stay in the dark.

The call went to voicemail immediately, which meant her phone was off, but I sent a text anyway. In the short time I'd known her, I'd never seen her turn the phone off, and the fact that it appeared to be powered down was starting to turn worry into something else.

I rubbed my jaw and told myself to think. If her phone was off, then she'd either turned it off, forgotten to charge it, had a phone problem...or she was in trouble. I had no way to check the first three directly, but I could do it indirectly.

She no longer had a roommate, but her apartment had a landline. I'd never seen her use it, but I knew a lot of apartments had kept landlines around, so I assumed hers still worked. I just had to find the number.

Now that I had something specific to do, I was able to focus. And multi-task. I called information while pulling up a search engine on my laptop. The search engine provided what I needed, and I made the call as I restlessly tapped my fingers on the table. If her phone had broken, that could explain why she was late since most people used their phones as alarm clocks.

I let the phone ring for nearly two solid minutes before finally giving up. She wasn't there. Even if she was in the shower, she would have heard the phone and gotten out surely.

But if she was there, why wouldn't she have used the

landline to call me? Unless she didn't have my number memorized. Or she'd simply forgotten about that phone. Either one made sense.

But, as much as I hated to admit it, the more likely scenario meant that something was really wrong.

My stomach churned as I pulled up a list of hospitals in New York. I had two more calls to make before I started on these, but whatever optimism I'd had was starting to fade.

"Bean Bodega, how can I help you?"

"Hello." I used my business voice, figuring it'd probably be more likely to get answers than if I was abrupt. "I sent my assistant to pick up some coffee early this morning. Short redhead. Irish."

"Yes, sir, she was here." The young woman on the other end sounded way too chipper for someone who worked in a service industry.

"Can you tell me when?"

"I'd just started my shift, so about eight thirty or so."

Shit. That sounded like the time she must've usually stopped there.

"But she didn't buy anything, sir, so there shouldn't be a problem with an order." A note of concern crept into the girl's voice.

"What do you mean she didn't buy anything?" I demanded.

"She came in just as I punched in, and I recognized her because I've served her before, but this time, she left before she could order." The words rushed out of her, as if she was afraid I'd lash out at her for something she had no control over.

"She left?"

"Yes, sir. I was filling a customer's order for a double expresso latte when I saw her walk out."

I knew better than to ask if she knew why. Bean Bodega was always packed in the morning. It was remarkable she'd noticed anything at all.

"Thank you," I said, ending the call before she could respond.

The fact that she'd been at the bodega for coffee told me she'd planned on coming into work. Something had changed though. It could have been anything from her feeling sick to deciding to get coffee somewhere else, or something outside might have gotten her attention, though what that could have been, I couldn't imagine.

Between the bodega and the studio, something had happened to keep her from coming into work.

Which meant I had other calls I needed to make.

I started with the hospitals, each call stretching my nerves and patience until they were both at a breaking point. Two hospitals told me that they had no one there by her name, but the others had refused to say anything without confirmation that I was a relative or spouse. Fortunately, I had people in influential places who owed me favors, including a private investigator.

"Max, it's Alix Wexler."

"Mr. Wexler, it's good to hear from you." As always, Max's voice was smooth, professional.

"Are you in New York right now?"

There was a slight pause that told me my question had come out a little more blunt than I'd intended.

"I am."

"Sorry," I apologized quickly. "I just have a case for you that needs top priority. If you're busy, I'll take a recommendation."

Another pause. I'd only met Max once or twice over the years, but my parents had sworn by his PI skills more than once when company employees or businesses had needed investigating. He was the best.

"I'll pay you double your usual rate," I offered.

"No need," he said. "I don't base case priority on who has the most money to throw around."

I closed my eyes and pinched the bridge of my nose. "I didn't mean to insult you," I said evenly. "My girlfriend is missing, and I need you to find her."

"Her name?"

"Sine McNiven."

"How long has she been missing?"

Even as I said it, I knew what he would say in response. "Since this morning."

"Was she taken off the street? From her home?"

At least he wasn't telling me I was overreacting. I gave him a quick rundown of everything I knew already.

"The two of you work together?"

His words were carefully chosen. He knew who I was because he knew my family, which meant he knew that I was a photographer.

"She's my assistant."

I knew better than to add that she was also modeling for me. He'd already think poorly of me for getting involved with an employee.

"When was the last time you spoke with her?"

I had to give him credit for keeping his judgment out of his voice. "Last night."

"And she didn't mention having anything else to do today?"

"No." I curbed my impatience, reminding myself that he could get information from hospitals that I couldn't. "And before you ask, we didn't have a fight. Things are going well between us."

"Have you contacted any family or friends to see if she talked to them?"

I pushed my hand through my hair. "Look, we've only been together for a little while. She's from Ireland, so I haven't even met her family." I didn't add that we hadn't even technically discussed whether or not we were referring to each other in boyfriend-girlfriend terms.

"That's why you called me."

"Exactly. Now are you going to take the case or not?"

"I will." There was a beat before he continued, "If you could send me a picture, I'll begin making the rounds. If I find her, I'll call you immediately."

After we finished up the rest of the details he needed from me, I started calling every other place I could think of. Restaurants we'd been together. Jean, though I kept my reasons for calling as vague as possible. Gilded Cage. Every business between here and the bodega.

Morgues.

As each called turned up nothing, I became more frustrated and less concerned, especially once I'd gotten the morgues out of the way. For three hours, I talked with people who were rude, bored, annoyed, and everything in-between, and I got nothing.

I tried calling her again, but there was still nothing. Every single one of them went straight to voicemail, where I left increasingly terse messages asking her to call me and let me know that she was all right.

As the afternoon went on without any progress, I had to face the fact that wherever Sine was, she didn't want me to find her. After all, how hard would it have been for her to call me and tell me what she was doing? Or a text? Or if her phone was dead, there were dozens of possible options, not the least of which was to stop here herself and explain why she'd blown off work. Blown off *me*.

It wasn't like she'd simply stood me up for a date. She had a job. Two of them, actually. Contracts that she'd signed. If nothing else, professionalism and courtesy weren't too much to ask for. I didn't know of any other employer who'd have spent the day looking for a missing employee rather than just firing them. Hospitalization, okay, that would be an understandable absence, but I was getting more and more confident that she wasn't hurt or in trouble.

She just hadn't cared enough about her job, or me, to tell me she wouldn't be coming in today.

As the fourth hour came and went without a word from her or from Max, I'd had enough. I dialed her number one final time.

Each word I said was flat and cold. I made no attempt to disguise my anger. I should have felt relief at ending things, but all I felt was mildly sick. I needed to get out of here. The studio held too many memories of her, and all I wanted to do right now was forget.

25

SINE

"Miss. Miss."

A woman's voice pulled me from a drug-induced slumber. For several long seconds, I couldn't remember where I was or why I needed to wake up. As I finally managed to raise my heavy eyelids, I saw a pair of near-black eyes watching me, and a pleasant smile on a plain face.

"We'll be making our descent shortly." She straightened and moved on.

My eyes followed her, my befuddled brain slowly taking in random details and piecing them together until I was able to remember that I was in an airplane. Once that clicked into place, everything else came flooding back and the fog that'd been in my head dissipated.

I was going home. Mam was in the hospital. I needed to get to her.

I rubbed my hands over my eyes, then ran my fingers

through my curls. They were probably sticking out at mad angles, but as long as I didn't look like the sort of random psycho who shouldn't be allowed into the country, I didn't care. I dug in my purse for some gum, then sat back and waited, my leg bouncing, fingers tapping.

"Nervous?"

I looked over at my seatmate. The elderly woman had been busy chatting with the person in front of us before I'd fallen asleep, but now her attention was focused on me.

Wonderful.

"Just eager to get on the ground," I said, making an attempt to smile.

"Coming home from a trip?" she asked, eyes lighting up when she heard my accent.

I shook my head. "I moved to New York for school and stayed."

Or, at least, that's how it'd been.

"Ah," she said. "Home for a visit then?"

This was not a conversation I wanted to have, but I couldn't figure out a way to politely ignore her question. I could, however, answer her honestly and hope it discouraged additional questions. "My mam's in the hospital."

"Oh, you poor dear." She put her hand on my arm as her eyes teared up.

For the next twenty-five minutes, she told me her life story, and I smiled and nodded, letting the words slip in one ear and out the other. She meant well, I supposed, thinking that her tale of woe offered me some sort of commiseration, but I didn't want to share what I was going through with a complete stranger. I had my siblings waiting for me, and they were the only ones I wanted to talk to about this. They would alleviate my guilt for not being there when it happened, for not being able to rush right to the hospital.

I still held it against myself though. Until the sleep aid I'd taken had pulled me under, I'd been going through every decision I'd made, every choice to stay in the States, every time I'd put schoolwork and saving for an apartment before trying to fly home for holidays, every missed opportunity to call or text or video chat. Each one of them ran through my head, one after another, mocking me, telling me what a horrible daughter I'd been. I should have gone to England. France. Scotland. Wales. Spain. A thousand different places that were closer than New York.

After college, I could have gone back. It hadn't been like I'd had some sort of glamorous job that I couldn't have found in Ireland. Even if I hadn't wanted to join in the family business, there were plenty of opportunities just as good as the temp work I'd been doing in New York.

Except I wouldn't have met Alix.

I bolted upright in my seat, startling the woman next to me.

Shit! Alix!

I'd completely forgotten to call him and tell him what happened. I'd been so busy and then security had taken forever. I'd barely made it onto the plane before being told to shut all electronics down. Everything else had slipped my mind. He must have been going crazy, not knowing where I'd been for the last ten hours.

I pulled my phone out of my purse. I'd turned it off rather than just putting it on airplane mode so I wouldn't drive myself crazy constantly checking it for updates that couldn't come through. Before I could turn it on, however, the flight attendant was back.

"Miss, you'll need to put that away." Her voice was polite, the words something she'd probably said a million times before.

I nodded and put it back in my bag. A few more minutes wouldn't hurt anything.

My nervous fidgeting grew worse the more time that passed. It felt like we'd been waiting forever, first to land, and then to come to a stop. I unbuckled as soon as the light went off, then gathered my things, ready to go as soon as we were allowed. Normally, I would've been the person who let others go first, but not today. It was almost midnight, but I had enough adrenaline coursing through my veins that I knew I'd be up for hours. Jet lag was going to hit me hard, but not before I had the chance to see for myself that Mam would be okay.

I'd debated the wisdom of checking luggage, but in the end, I managed to get enough for a week crammed into a single carry-on, so I went straight from the plane to the place where Colin was waiting. He'd been dating Donald for three years now, but I'd only met him once when he'd come with my brother to my graduation.

As I paused by the door, I turned on my phone. Colin

was supposed to text me when he arrived so I'd know where to find him, but I didn't see a message from him yet. What I did see was a dozen missed messages, almost as many missed calls and voicemails. All from Alix.

Fuck.

I scanned through the messages, frowning as the tone went from concerned to annoyed. He wasn't exactly being rude, but they were shitty enough that by the time I moved on to the voicemails, I was ready to give him a piece of my mind when I called him back.

The first couple voicemails were similar to the texts, full of worry about why I hadn't come to work or let him know where I was. With every new one, my heart sank, and my stomach churned. Then I reached the last.

Miss McNiven, as you have failed to show courtesy and respect toward your job, or to me, there is no need to contact me. You are in breach of contract, and your employment has been terminated. Your things will be delivered to your apartment. Should you have any questions, please contact my lawyer to discuss the penalties for breaking your contracts. Good day.

What. The. Fuck.

I stared at my phone as if that would make it less awful. Okay, I'd made a mess of things by not calling him before I left, for certain, but he hadn't even given me the benefit of the doubt for twenty-four hours. Apparently, if I wasn't in the hospital, then whatever reason I could have had for not contacting him wasn't good enough. I'd inconvenienced *him*. Worried *him*. Made him waste *his* time.

The tension that had been building inside me didn't

break in a flood of tears. No, he didn't deserve me to cry over him. Not when my mother was lying in a hospital bed. He didn't know that, but he'd made assumptions, not based on what he knew of me, but on what he considered important.

He didn't know me at all.

Everything I thought we had was now tarnished by the realization that it – that *I* – had never meant as much to him as he had to me.

A text alert came up from Colin, telling me he'd just arrived.

Fuck Alix.

If he didn't have the decency to not believe the worst, then he wasn't the man I thought he was.

My fingers shook as I tapped out a response. Once sent, I would put him aside and focus on the reason I was here.

I *have no questions. You made yourself entirely clear in your final message. Should you wish to retain my last paycheck, consider it compensation for my breach of contract. We're done.*

I deleted the message two days after I received it, but it didn't really matter because I'd read it so many times that I had it memorized. It played through my head whether I wanted it to or not. Morning, noon, and night. When I was showering. Eating. Driving. Standing. Sitting.

I hadn't realized how much I'd been unconsciously planning a future with Sine until she was gone. Independence Day was tomorrow. Usually, the guys and I went to the Hamptons. We weren't huge partiers, but we sometimes had people come with us, sometimes we didn't. This year, however, Erik wanted to be with Tanya, which made things awkward for the rest of us. Reb because he and

Mitzi weren't together anymore. Me because of...*her*. And then Jace called tonight and said that he wanted to work on something new and wouldn't be able to make it.

I stared up at the ceiling the same as I had for almost six days straight. The night I'd gotten the text from her, I drank myself into a stupor, her last two words echoing in my head until I finally passed out. I hadn't really moved much since then.

I certainly hadn't been working.

I thought I'd been blocked before, but it was nothing like now. I couldn't see anything but her.

And I didn't know how to stop.

TODAY MADE it five weeks since Sine had disappeared. Five weeks since I felt like the world no longer had any color, any meaning. I'd gone through all the stages. Denial. Anger. Bargaining. Depression. Acceptance.

I looked at my reflection as I crossed in front of a mirror and winced. Okay, so maybe I was still in the depression stage. I rubbed my hand over my jaw. I hadn't shaved in days, and the only reason I'd done it then had been because Erik had threatened to kick my ass if I missed another night at the club.

Even well-groomed, I hadn't been able to fool my friends. The worst part was, it wasn't just me who was miserable. Reb was too. And Jace was distracted. Erik was preoccupied with Tanya.

Being with them at the club should have felt like getting back to normal. And that should have been what I wanted. A life like the one I'd had before she came along. Physically satisfying sex that didn't have strings attached. Focusing on my career. A world that had been simpler.

But it wasn't enough.

Having been with Sine, I couldn't go back to the way things had been. I wasn't the same man. She'd connected with me on a level I hadn't known existed.

Or I thought she had.

But I'd been wrong.

She couldn't have written that text if she felt the same way I did. Had. Not *did*. Because I was over her.

Except even now, as I stood in the middle of my studio, thoughts of her kept creeping in. Memories.

The blank space on the walls didn't help. I'd torn down every picture of her. Since then, I'd been trying to find something to replace them, but I was worse off than I had been before I met Sine. Then, I hadn't known what I wanted to do. I'd been in a creative blind spot.

Now, I knew what I wanted to do, but I couldn't see anyone else in her place. Every time I tried, I found flaws, reasons why none of the models I'd worked with in the past could possibly make my vision come alive.

The only thing worse than not having any idea of what I wanted to do, was knowing *exactly* what I wanted but not being able to do it.

"You've been dodging my calls, Alix."

The familiar voice made me turn, but I already knew it

wasn't the person I wanted it to be. Or didn't want it to be. I was still torn as to which I wanted more. To be able to move on and forget about her, or see her again so I could have closure.

At the moment, however, neither one was an option.

"Giselle." I didn't even have the energy to attempt a smile, even if I'd wanted to be pleasant to the woman.

She strolled toward me, her blood-red lips curved into what I was certain she intended to be impossibly seductive.

It just made me more tired.

"I was disappointed when I didn't hear from you," she said, stroking a hand down my arm.

She wore a skimpy top, the sort of miniskirt that barely covered her ass, and a pair of six-inch heels. Every inch of her screamed for attention, for people to notice her.

I stepped out of arms reach from her, but she didn't seem discouraged. "I thought you'd found someone else for your great new series, but then I overheard some other models saying that you haven't had anyone come in for more than a month. I thought you were still hoping that those pictures you took with that assistant of yours would become something. Then I heard she was gone too."

My hands curled into fists for a moment, but the flicker of anger that went through me burned out almost as quickly as it came.

"I'm not feeling particularly creative today," I said quietly. "Please see yourself out."

Her eyes widened, then narrowed. "There were rumors going around that you'd fallen for her. That assistant of yours. Was that the reason why you let her model for you?" Her beautiful face twisted into something ugly. "I guess I just got it backwards, right? You don't sleep with your models. You just let the women you fuck become your models."

"Leave, Giselle. Before you say something you regret." I meant the threat, but there was no heat behind it.

She raised an eyebrow. "What, exactly, is that supposed to mean?"

I sighed and scratched at my beard. "It means that I'm not interested in you, Giselle. And I would hate to put the word out that you were behaving unprofessionally toward a photographer."

She threw a couple choice words at me on her way out, but I didn't acknowledge them. I didn't really care what she thought of me. I didn't need or want her approval. I was having a difficult time wanting anything actually.

Sure, I ate, drank. I went through the motions. But that's all they were. Motions.

I scratched my cheek again, unsure of how much time had passed since Giselle had stormed out.

This beard itched like a motherfucker. I needed to shave.

I turned off the lights as I left, more out of habit than anything else. If I didn't snap out of this soon, I was going to sell the studio and talk to my cousin Izett about what I could do within the company. If I couldn't have what I wanted, I might as well make myself useful to the family.

I'd come back tomorrow and see if anything changed.

I wasn't hopeful, but it was something to do.

27
=====

SINE

I 'd only been gone a little over a month, but it felt like
a lifetime.

"Coming or going?" The balding man in the aisle
seat gave me a friendly smile. His accent marked him as
being from Glasgow. "Are you going to visit or coming
home?"

I answered honestly, my voice soft, "I'm not sure."

He gave me an odd look, but I was already turning my
attention back toward the window. It was evening, but
since it was August, it was still light enough for me to see
out the window. The Statue of Liberty was visible in the
distance, reminding me of the first time I saw it.

Then, I'd been full of hope, eager to start the new
adventure. Now, as I looked at the city I once considered
home, all I felt was dread.

Staying in Ireland hadn't been appealing either. Not
with everyone giving me sideways looks, wondering just

how much of the truth I was telling about my life in America. I hadn't exactly given anyone much to go on either. I'd said it was because I wanted to focus on Mam, but it was a weak-sounding excuse that I doubted most of my family had believed. Once everything had started getting back to normal, my reason for being there faded.

Mam had been in the hospital only for a couple days, but the doctors had wanted to run some tests when they hadn't been able to find an initial cause for her passing out. Of course, I stayed to see through the results, which had basically said she needed to change her diet, and then I'd spent time with each of my siblings and their families. But there was only so much time someone could claim to be taking as a vacation. I'd needed to make a choice.

Not that *there* really was a choice as far as I was concerned.

I couldn't stay, not when I'd left things unfinished here.

Not when I didn't know what I wanted.

The descent into JFK was smooth and drama free, but it didn't ease the knots in my stomach. The text message I'd sent to Alix ending things had shown as being read, but he hadn't sent back a response. I hadn't expected him to, not after I told him we were through, but that lack of expectation hadn't explained itself to my heart.

I missed him.

As hacked off as I'd been at him, I was hurt that he hadn't replied, hadn't fought for me.

Part of it was on me though too. I'd been on an emotional edge when I'd gotten his texts and voicemails, and I'd reacted impulsively rather than thinking things through like I usually did. I'd let what happened with my mom cloud my judgment when it came to dealing with Alix, and I shouldn't have. I should have called him and explained what'd happened. Then, if he'd still behaved like a total asshole, my anger could have been justified.

"Here you go, lass." The Scot pulled my bag from the overhead compartment and handed it to me. "You be safe."

"Thank you," I said as I took my bag. I kept my head down as I followed the other passengers off the plane.

I didn't have anyone waiting for me since I hadn't told anyone I was coming back. Not that I would've had anyone to call. I'd burned whatever ties I had to people here when I left without an explanation. I made my way to the exit where taxis would be parked, and as I stepped outside, the heat hit me hard enough to make me stagger back a step. Humidity so thick that it felt like breathing water. The cloying smell of pavement and diesel that would include other scents as I went into Manhattan.

I was back.

No more putting off thinking about it or pretending that it wasn't happening. The time I spent in Ireland felt like some sort of dream, an out of body experience. I'd focused on my family and hadn't let myself think about New York too much. I hadn't been able to put it completely out of my mind, but it'd still been enough to keep me from having to acknowledge the full extent of what awaited me until this very moment.

The little bit of psychology I knew said that the sense

of smell was the one most powerfully linked to memories. One whiff of something could bring back a host of memories and emotions, and with every breath I took, I was pulled back into the life I had abandoned five weeks ago.

I scrubbed at my cheeks, wiping away the evidence of the tears that had spilled over without my consent. I'd spent too much time over the past five weeks crying to start it all over again now. Once I was safely in my own apartment again, I might allow myself to give in, but I wouldn't do it here.

I opened the door to the cab and slid my bag into the backseat next to me. I gave him the address and settled back in the seat. I'd arrived not too long after the worst of rush hour traffic, so the streets were still going to be crowded, but as much as I wanted to be back in my own place, I was grateful for the slow pace.

My landlord had been understanding when I'd called to tell him my predicament. He'd agreed to hold my apartment as long as I kept him in the loop about when I'd be coming back, and I'd sent him a letter last week with August's rent, letting him know I planned to return this month. That, plus a plane ticket back, had drained my bank account. I had enough left for the necessities, but I'd need to start looking for work right away.

I paid the driver, then headed to the door. I rubbed my palms against my jeans and flexed my fingers. My heart thudded against my chest as adrenaline flooded through me. I could have waited to do this, gathered my courage. Called first.

If I put it off, though, things would only get harder. I needed to have this done so I could start planning for my future.

I knocked and waited. It was possible he wasn't here, but I was hoping he was. If not, I'd have to figure out a way to get past the doorman at his building, and that would just make matters even more complicated than they already were.

After a couple minutes, I reached for the door. If it was locked, I'd go to his apartment. The door opened easily though, and I stepped inside. I knew there was a chance I'd be interrupting Alix and some woman, but if that was the case, then I deserved the heartache such a sight would offer. What had happened between us was as much my fault as it was his.

The first thing I felt when I saw him standing by the table was relief that he was alone. Then I really saw him, and a stab of pain went through my heart. Even from his profile, I could see dark smudges under his eyes. A bit of scruff on his usually close-shaven face. Clothes rumpled.

As that all registered, I also saw that there were no pictures on the walls. No equipment or props to be seen. The place was virtually empty.

"Alix." I said his name softly, not wanting to startle him, but he jumped anyway.

He turned the rest of the way toward me, eyes widening.

Before he could say anything at all, I blurted out the words that had brought me here straight from the airport.

The words that were the reason I hadn't had a choice about coming back to New York. The words that had changed everything for me...and would do the same for him.

"I'm pregnant."

28

ALIX

I'd come back to the studio to pack things up. It'd been more than a month since I produced anything decent. I'd never gone that long without taking a single picture, not since I first started my own professional studio. I wasn't giving up, I told myself. I was just taking a break until I figured out what I would do next.

The common sense part of me knew that I was just making excuses. This wasn't simply a loss of inspiration. It was a loss of desire. All I'd ever wanted to do from the moment I picked up my first camera was to be a photographer.

Until now.

Everything was numb. Gray.

And I was pretty sure my friends were going to stage an intervention for me in the near future if I didn't snap out of it soon.

That was the main reason why I didn't answer the door

when someone knocked. I loved my cousin, but I hadn't been able to stomach being around Erik this past month. He was too fucking happy. Even when he and Tanya were arguing, he was obnoxious. He said it was because he knew that what they had was stronger than a disagreement.

Bastard.

I heard the door open but ignored it. Whoever it was could go and–

"Alix."

I jumped. Fuck me. It was *her*.

I turned around even as my brain kept trying to tell me that I'd imagined it. That it couldn't possibly be Sine. She was gone. She'd left me.

But it *was* her.

Some part of my brain registered all of the physical things. Her wild curls. The bruised-looking flesh under her eyes. Her clothes hanging on her. How the skin on her face looked stretched too tight over her bones. The way her once sparkling eyes were dull.

But most of all, I was consumed by the fact that my heart seemed to have stopped, frozen. My lungs burning as I forgot to breathe.

I only had a few seconds for it all to sink in because then...

"I'm pregnant."

I gave my head a shake because I must have heard her incorrectly. There was no way she was pregnant. None.

"I'm sorry to be blurting it out like that," she continued,

her accent thicker than it had been when she'd...left. She twisted her hands together and took a step forward. "I meant to be...I mean...dammit."

Seeing her flustered broke me out of my daze. "Why?" The question came out flat. "Why would you leave if you're..." I couldn't finish the question. Saying the word would make it real.

"I didn't know," she said. Her eyes flicked to mine for a moment. "When I left, I didn't know. I found out on Monday but didn't want to be telling you over the phone."

"You didn't seem to have a problem telling me we were done via text, so I have a hard time believing that you can't give news over the phone." I sounded petty, but the filter between my brain and my mouth wasn't really working. It'd stalled somewhere around *pregnant* and hadn't come back online yet.

I waited for her to come back with something sarcastic or snarky or angry. Anything that meant we could have it out and finally get some closure. Move on.

Or, as much as we could move on when a baby was in the mix.

Baby.

Shit.

How in the *fuck* had *that* happened?

"That day – the day I left – I was on my way into work." Her voice stayed the same. Quiet. Even.

Emotionless.

"While I was at the bodega, my brother called. My mother had passed out and was rushed to the hospital."

Shit.

"I rushed home, packed, then went straight to the airport. There was a cancellation almost right away."

My stomach continued to drop, and my heart followed.

"I was on the phone with Donald until I stepped onto the plane...and turned my phone off."

By the time I'd realized she was missing, she'd already been in the air.

With her phone off.

Because her mom had been rushed to the hospital.

I was a complete ass.

"I should have called you, I know," she continued. "But I didn't think of it with all the rush of getting on the plane. All I could think of was getting home to Mam."

The worst kind of ass.

"We were landing when I remembered. As soon as I turned on my phone, I..." She swallowed hard. "I saw your messages."

Petulant, childish messages.

She risked another look at me, and I wondered if she could see the guilt written across my face.

"I accept my part for what happened between us," she said. "And I'm not here to be asking for anything. I have no expectations–"

"I'm so sorry." I crossed the distance between us, my heart ready to beat out of my chest. "This is all my fault. I fucked up. I should have trusted you, trusted that there was a good reason–"

She shook her head, fatigue written on every line of

her body. "Water under the bridge. No need to dredge up the past."

I reached out for her, then thought better of it. She probably didn't want me to touch her, not after everything I'd done.

But I'd be damned if I stopped trying.

"I mean it, Sine. I am so sorry. I never should have said those things." My heart twisted again. I wasn't numb anymore. I was feeling, and it sucked. "I was an asshole."

Not even a hint of a smile.

"Please, Sine." My voice cracked. "I was wrong. Forgive me."

It was a plea, not a command.

"Only if you forgive me for not telling you."

I couldn't stop myself from taking her hands. Despite the heat outside, her hands were cold. "You didn't do anything wrong. You were thinking about your mom. As you should have been. You didn't deserve to have to deal with my shit on top of everything else."

Her bottom lip trembled, and I released her hands to cup her face between my palms. I hated seeing her upset, and hated even more that I was responsible for it.

"Whatever you think you should feel guilty for, don't. You did nothing wrong. I was a bastard for how I behaved."

I took a step back.

"Please tell me that your mother's okay." If her mom wasn't...I'd never forgive myself for putting the extra stress on Sine.

"She is."

Some of the life seemed to be coming back into Sine's eyes. That was good. I needed her to be herself again...before we talked about that *other* thing she said.

"And I forgive you."

Relief flooded through me, almost making my knees weak.

"But there is a question I'd like you to answer."

I nodded, wondering if I should ask her to go somewhere else for us to have the baby discussion.

Baby.

Fuck.

I was going to be–

"What's going to happen now? With us, I mean."

Shit.

29

SINE

I knew we had to discuss the baby, but I needed to know where things stood between us. That would tell me what to expect when we discussed his involvement. I promised myself that I'd accept whatever he wanted.

He was quiet for several seconds, each one stretching out until I was worried that I'd asked the wrong thing.

"What is it you want to happen, Sine?" His voice was soft.

My pulse hadn't slowed from the moment I knocked on his door, but it seemed to beat double-time at the question. I'd given him my forgiveness, and he seemed to genuinely care about what happened, but I wouldn't be fooled into mistaking wishful thinking for something more solid.

Coming here was a risk, not only because I hadn't been certain of the welcome I'd receive, especially once I shared my news, but because I knew he had the power to break my heart.

But I also knew that if I didn't take a chance now, I'd regret it. I'd never been a coward, and I'd never forgive myself if I turned into one now.

I had to lay it all out there.

"I want..." I laid my hand on my stomach. It was still flat, but I'd found myself standing that way from the moment I'd seen that plus sign. As if I could feel my son or daughter already there, growing inside me.

Alix's gaze followed my hand, and I watched the expression on his face change, as if somehow my gesture made it real to him, the same way the test had made it for me.

"I want us to be together," I said the words simply, forcing myself not to rush through them. "I want us to see if this works. You and me and..."

"Our baby," he finished.

I nodded, then forced myself to add, "If that isn't what you'll be wanting, I'll understand. And I won't be asking you for anything, should you not wish to be a part–"

I lost the rest of what I intended to say when his mouth came down on mine. I felt the hunger in his kiss all the way down to my bones, and the desire I'd been keeping down came rushing forward. I grabbed the front of his shirt, holding him close, letting everything I felt pour into him. If I walked away with my heart in shreds, I would do it with everything left on the table.

He pulled back after a moment, then rested his forehead against mine.

"You asked me what I want," he said as he cupped my face. "I want *you*."

He dropped his hand between us and placed it on my stomach. The heat of his palm warmed me through the thin cotton of my t-shirt.

"I want *us*."

A surge of hope went through me, strong enough that I couldn't quite suppress it. "I want to be certain I understand you..."

He held my chin in one hand, keeping our eyes locked. "Then let me be clear. I want you in my life. I want our child in my life. I want it to be *our* life. Our family."

If I was a different sort of woman, I might have melted into a puddle after hearing those words. But I didn't melt. What I did was take a shaky breath, then let it out with all the tension I'd been holding.

"I love you, Sine." He brushed his lips across mine. "And I want you to be mine."

A lump formed in my throat, and I felt tears burning in my eyes.

Apparently, I *was* that sort of woman.

Damned hormones.

"I am yours," I managed to whisper. "For as long as you'll want me."

"Forever," he said earnestly. "I want you forever."

He kissed me again, hands sliding around my waist, and then down to cup my behind through my jeans. He pulled me tight against him, and I wound my arms around his neck, needing to feel the hard press of his body to assure me that I wasn't dreaming, wasn't imagining his words. I hadn't let myself hope for this, no matter how much I wanted it.

I dug my hands into his hair, pushed myself up on my toes as I nipped at his bottom lip. He groaned, his hands squeezing my ass, and a bolt of desire went through me, the sort of desire that only he could make me feel.

My memory hadn't done reality any justice.

Emboldened, I tugged at his shirt, needing more. He took a step back, hands closing around my wrists. I frowned, confused.

"I thought – I mean–"

"I want to," he said quickly. "I just..." He looked down for a moment, and when he looked up again, his expression was sheepish. "I don't want to hurt you."

Now I was even more confused.

Until I suddenly realized what he meant. Then, I was amused.

"You won't." I stepped into him so that our combined hands were caught between us. I smiled up at him. "Not for real."

I could see the struggle on his face, and I pulled one hand free from his grasp, reaching up to brush my fingers over his eyebrow. He made a sound in the back of his throat as I rested my palm against his cheek. He closed his eyes, leaning into my touch.

"When I say that I want you, I mean *all* of you," I

assured him. I reached down and ran my fingers over the erection straining against his zipper. "Now, I don't know about you, but I would like to be picking things up where we left off."

His response was to pull his shirt over his head, then reach for mine, yanking it up and tossing it to the floor. His eyes never left mine, not even as he went to his knees in front of me. Neither of us spoke as he helped me out of my jeans, or when he gently kissed my stomach. Everything else that'd happened between us faded away as he rested his cheek against my bare skin. I ran my fingers through his hair, the heat between us settling to a quiet simmer for a few peaceful moments.

Then he kissed his way across my stomach, just above the waistband of my panties. I made a soft noise as the sensations tickled, but I didn't want him to stop. Especially not when he gripped my knee and draped my leg over his shoulder. I put a hand on his other shoulder, balancing myself as he pulled the panties to one side and put his mouth on me.

My eyes wanted to close as he moved his tongue over me, dipping down before coming back up to circle my clit, but I kept them open, not wanting to miss a moment of this man, on his knees, pleasuring me. Worshipping me.

He put a hand on the small of my back as his tongue flicked back and forth in rapid succession, each touch the perfect combination of friction and pressure.

"Ah..." I made a strangled sound as my muscles tensed. "Alix." His name came out in a whimper as I climaxed.

"I've got you," he murmured, the air ghosting across my skin.

The shiver sent another ripple of pleasure through me, a ripple that kept going as Alix placed my foot on the floor. He stood as he ran his hands over my ribcage, under my breasts, and moved his thumbs over my nipples. They hardened under my bra, and I moaned as he covered one with his mouth, teasing it through the fabric.

"Alix." I tugged on his hair. "Please."

He raised his head, a glint in his eyes. "Impatient, aren't you?"

I glared at him, then laughed as he swept me up in his arms. He didn't take me far, just over to the couch where he laid me down, stripping off my panties and bra before taking a step back to remove the last of his clothes.

I reached out my hands to him, and he took them as he moved to kneel between my legs. The couch was narrow, but it was enough for what we were going to do, and that was all that mattered at the moment.

He shifted his grasp so that he was holding both my wrists in one hand. As he stretched out on top of me, he put my arms over my head, holding them firm against the arm of the couch. His free hand clutched my hip, as he rocked against me. The tip of his cock slipped over my wet folds, then between them to nudge against my clit.

He hesitated, gaze searching my face for something.

"I love you," I said. "Alix Wexler. All of you. Faults. Strengths." I wiggled my hands. "Kinks."

He smiled then, leaning down to take my mouth as he

surged forward, locking us together in one smooth thrust. My body arched up to meet his, to find the completion that only he could bring. We moved together in perfect rhythm, each push and pull relentlessly driving us toward the same goal.

His tongue plundered my mouth, thoroughly owning it as much as his body owned mine. He owned everything. My heart. Mind. Soul. Everything. But as our release crashed into us, I saw the truth in his eyes. I owned him as well.

It wasn't until several minutes had passed, and I was tucked back against him, his fingers tracing patterns on my stomach, that he broke the silence.

"Marry me."

We'd known each other only two months and had been apart for half of them. Of course, there was only one answer I could give.

30

SINE

The late summer weather decided to cut us a break, which meant I wasn't sweltering in my simple pale green dress. I didn't wear many dresses, but I knew that my mother would never forgive me if she saw pictures of today with me in shorts. She was already disapproving of the whole thing as it was.

Even though I'd discovered I was pregnant while still in Ireland, I hadn't told my family then. I'd wanted to have a plan in place before breaking the news. Besides, Alix had deserved to know first.

When I called them the day after Alix and I reconciled, I'd been able to tell them that Alix had proposed, and that I'd accepted. I'd also told them that we'd be making it legal at the courthouse in only two weeks. Mam hadn't been happy, but when I'd assured her that I'd bring him to meet the family as soon as we were able, she'd been mollified. A bit at least.

Despite the fact that we weren't standing in a good Catholic church, Mam would want pictures. And we would want to show pictures to our son or daughter one day.

So, I was wearing a dress.

But that wasn't really the main thing on my mind. I couldn't take my eyes off Alix. He was wearing a suit at my request rather than a tuxedo, but I wasn't fool enough to believe that the suit wasn't the kind tailor-made at a price that I didn't want to think about.

And I wanted to peel off every expensive layer and trace his abs with my tongue. Move my mouth lower...

Dammit.

Heat suffused my cheeks. I'd been blessed to not have much morning sickness, but I'd discovered a more unexpected symptom when Alix and I had made love my first night back.

I wanted him all the time.

Insatiably.

As in I couldn't even sit next to him and watch a movie without touching him. Sliding my hand up his leg, feeling his thigh muscles tense and bunch. Unzipping his pants and taking him in my mouth.

The night he proposed, we stayed in my apartment, but the next day, we'd taken my things to his place.

And then christened every room. Twice.

He'd rebuffed my attempts to get him to join me in the shower this morning, saying that we'd be late if we showered together, and I'd had to admit that he was right.

That didn't mean I planned on waiting until after the party I knew Alix's friends had planned for us before we left for our honeymoon. If I had to, I'd settle for a quickie in a closet or in the limo.

And I'd come prepared.

I let a little smirk into my smile as he stretched out his hand. I took it and stepped up next to him.

"You're up to something," he said under his breath.

"Perhaps," I answered coyly.

"And what would that be?" He leaned closer so that our conversation was still private. "Perhaps something for the honeymoon?"

I shook my head and snuck a glance at the Justice of the Peace who was still searching in his desk for something, "Since you refused to assist me in getting dressed this morning, I may have neglected to put on...everything."

His eyes widened, then narrowed as they slid over me, sending my pulse racing. "Are you telling me that under that dress..."

"I suppose you'll need to find out."

His fingers tightened around mine as he pulled me closer to him so that his mouth was pressed against my ear. "When we get in the limo, I'm going to pull up that dress, and if I find you bare, you'll be in for a punishment."

I shivered as he pulled back. "Yes, please."

His eyes darkened. "Let's get this started."

Even when the Justice began the familiar ceremony, I didn't take my gaze from Alix's. The words would make it official, but I already knew that he was my future. My forever.

I must have said the right things at the right times because before I knew it, he was kissing me, and the guys were whistling. Someone cleared their throat, and Alix broke the kiss, his eyes shining, a smile stretched from ear to ear. His thumb moved back and forth over my rings as he raised my hand to brush a kiss across my knuckles.

"I love you, Sine Wexler."

"And I love you," I replied. "But don't think this gets you off the hook for the big Catholic wedding Mam is planning for next month. The whole family is looking forward to meeting you."

He swallowed hard, a bit of anxiety showing in his eyes. "How many brothers do you have again?"

I gave him a wry smile. "Six. But it's not the brothers you need to be worrying about."

"Ex?"

I shook my head and laughed. "You knocked up a staunch Irish Catholic's daughter out of wedlock, and you'll have to be answering to Mam about that."

The End

The Billionaire's Muse will be back in November in a third book, this time following Jace.

ALSO BY M. S. PARKER

The Rockstar's Virgin

SEALionaire

Make Me Yours

The Billionaire's Mistress

Con Man Box Set

HERO Box Set

A Legal Affair Box Set

The Champ

The Client

Indecent Encounter

Dom X Box Set

Unlawful Attraction Box Set

Chasing Perfection Box Set

Blindfold Box Set

Club Prive Box Set

The Pleasure Series Box Set

Exotic Desires Box Set

Pure Lust Box Set

Casual Encounter Box Set

Sinful Desires Box Set

Twisted Affair Box Set

Serving HIM Box Set

ACKNOWLEDGMENTS

First, I would like to thank all of my readers. Without you, my books would not exist. I truly appreciate each and every one of you.

A big "thanks" goes out to all the Facebook fans, street team, beta readers, and advanced reviewers. You are a HUGE part of the success of all my series.

I have to thank my PA, Shannon Hunt. Without you my life would be a complete and utter mess. Also a big thank you goes out to my editor Lynette and my wonderful cover designer, Sinisa. You make my ideas and writing look so good.

ABOUT THE AUTHOR

M. S. Parker is a USA Today Bestselling author and the author of the Erotic Romance series, Club Privè and Chasing Perfection.

Living in Las Vegas, she enjoys sitting by the pool with her laptop writing on her next spicy romance.

Growing up all she wanted to be was a dancer, actor or author. So far only the latter has come true but M. S. Parker hasn't retired her dancing shoes just yet. She is still waiting for the call for her to appear on Dancing With The Stars.

When M. S. isn't writing, she can usually be found reading– oops, scratch that! She is always writing.

For more information:

www.msparker.com
msparkerbooks@gmail.com

Made in the USA
Monee, IL
05 March 2021

62026870R00125